Murder Calls at Shadow Falls

An Olivia Twist Cozy Mystery Book #1

Irene Jorgensen

D1714546

Apatite Publishing

Get Your FREE Novella

A persistent grandmother. A twenty-five year old death. And a shaky clue to prove it was murder.

Just when Olivia thought she was well on her way to redemption...

...she gets hit with a request to solve an old murder by channeling the dead.

How's a good-hearted fake psychic supposed to do that?

Get a free copy of *Suspect Guests and an Unwelcome Request* at IreneJorgensen.com when you join my newsletter. You'll also get cozy email stories, opportunities for more books (mine and other authors), updates, the occasional recipe and cat picture.

Chapter 1

RETURNING TO SHADOW FALLS for an afternoon to visit my grandmother—what were the odds I'd get caught?

The risks seemed minimal.

Something I mulled over, every time I opened one of my grandmother's emails, which always contained an invitation for tea.

GG, my grandmother, refused to stop attempting to lure me home. She claimed my good qualities far outweighed my one teensy-weensy crime. (Her words, not mine.)

I almost deleted her latest unopened email.

As I hovered the mouse over the tiny trash can icon, it seemed like some invisible force moved my hand to open the email instead. Sure enough, another tea invitation, although a more formal one.

Meg Twist requests the company of her granddaughter Olivia Twist for afternoon tea at 2:00 p.m. on Sunday, April 14th.

Honestly. Did GG think I'd forgotten I was her granddaughter?

Argh. How I missed her and my hometown with a yearning I'd not expected when I'd left (okay, snuck out) four years earlier—on the day I will forever call Dark Monday.

Returning simply wasn't an option, not after what I'd done.

If time travel existed and one could go back to undo those wrong turns, I'd settle for undoing just one. That one.

About to decline GG's invitation, I noticed her postscript.

P.S. Please come to tea. I'd like to see you one more time. I'm sick and might die sooner rather than later.

Sick? Might die?

It took a few moments for the shock to recede enough for logic to surface. Was it possible my melodramatic grandmother had used a sniffle to lure me home? Oh, yeah.

Still...what if this was something more serious? What if she was close to death, and I'd let my fears and shame prevent me from seeing her one last time? On top of everything else on my conscience, I didn't know if I could survive abandoning the woman who had saved me.

This time, I didn't mull over the risks. I answered yes.

Then I devised a plan to minimize the possibility of anyone recognizing me—like learning professional makeup techniques (not cheap) and wearing a bright color (red) I never wore in the past.

On the morning of April fourteenth, I left Boston early, drove just under the speed limit during the six-hour trip to western New York, and arrived at the outskirts of Shadow Falls at noon.

I'd steeled myself for the onslaught of memories. And just as I'd feared, images of Jake O'Grady popped up at my first sighting of the lake. Him getting out of the water. Pushing wet, dark brown hair off his face. Laughing slate gray eyes. How those eyes had turned somber when he told me he'd enlisted. His earnest expression, as he assured me, *promised* me he'd always come home to me. How I'd clung to that promise, however unrealistic it might have been.

Then Dark Monday—the day my alleged boss had stolen from my team just before I found out Jake had gone missing in action. How I couldn't bear the memories, the reality of living here without him, so I'd taken money to get out of town. Then when a semblance of sanity had returned, the distress my theft had caused. How it had destroyed friendships. How it had ruined my life.

How I deserved the subsequent anguish.

Not wanting to turn into a blubbering mess in my car, I shoved the memories into the darkest shadows of my mind before I lost all energy to execute my plan.

My plan? Drive straight to GG's house, get her to confess she'd used emotional blackmail to lure me home, have tea, then leave Shadow Falls, never to return.

As much as I deserved to suffer for my theft, I didn't want that suffering to include prison. I figured my anguish and loneliness were punishment enough. (Although, I'm sure others might disagree.)

I stopped at the side of the road to button my new red spring coat, tuck a few brunette hairs under my platinum blonde wig and reapply lip plumper and blush. Donning my sunglasses, I practiced my British accent, which I'd perfected listening to royalty on YouTube videos.

If my plan went awry and I ran into anyone I knew, my disguise and accent were good enough to fool even my close friends, now ex-friends.

I let out a long breath, stepped on the gas of my old, black Toyota Echo, the car I'd bought after I left town, then pulled over a half mile down the road to stare at the sign for the town's annual spring fair. It was today of all days.

A yearning for the good old days grew into a sudden urge to stroll the fairgrounds and take pictures. Sure, a risky, some might say stupid, move. Except, the nostalgia far outweighed the fear someone might recognize me. And after all, I was in disguise and barely recognized myself through the heavy makeup. What were the odds anyone else would?

I stepped on the gas, reached downtown Shadow Falls a

minute later, then drank in the sights as if it were my first time here.

Crowds wandered along the storefronts' wide cobblestone sidewalk on the downtown strip where the brick stores butted up against each other plaza style. No fast-food joints here. A steak and seafood restaurant, a hair salon, a bookstore, a hardware store, several boutiques, the old video store that had sat vacant for years, and—I slowed the car. The video store had a For Sale sign in one of the windows. Huh.

Next to the video store was the café bakery. My ex-best friend Annie Parker had wanted to buy it when it came on the market. Because of me, she had lost it. The pang in my heart still pierced as if it had happened yesterday.

My left temple itched near the edge of my wig. I scratched as I drove onto the public lot by the lake and parked close to the waterfalls.

What a perfect day to wander through the spring fair. Only a few puffy clouds dotted the sky. With my tote bag slung over my shoulder, phone in hand, ready to take pictures, I climbed out of my car. Carnival music drowned out the crash of the nearby falls.

On my way to the fair set up in the park, I stopped for a few seconds to gaze across the bay where my grandmother still lived. How sick was she? Maybe I should go straight to her. I checked my watch—almost time for GG's nap. I'd wait because nothing turned her into Grumpy Granny faster than an interrupted afternoon nap.

I passed parents herding excited children. A couple holding hands sauntered past me, and once again, Jake crossed my mind. Maybe a stroll down fairground lane was a bad idea. I pressed on to capture moments of happier yesterdays.

Shadow Falls' simple fairs consisted of food vendors and tables laden with stuff for sale. Vintage dresses (read: old) hanging on a portable clothes rack. A stall filled with upcycled furniture painted with green vines and purple pansies. Mop dolls with button eyes from the same old lady who had come from out of town to set up her stall every year for as long as I could remember. How Annie and I had loved those dolls.

Food vendors shouted at passersby to taste their wares. Deep-fried donuts. Popcorn. Cotton candy. The smells—a mishmash of hometown carnival comfort.

I froze when I came face-to-face with one of my friends from whom I'd stolen money.

Daisy glanced at me and did a doubletake. Was it my hideous makeup? Or had she recognized me? She stopped and peered at me.

My mind spun. If I bolted to the car, I'd be out of town in less than five minutes. But what about my sick grandmother? I needed to see her. If Daisy called the sheriff and he showed up at GG's house, I'd hide in the cellar.

I was about to turn and run when Daisy touched my arm. "Are you all right, ma'am? You don't look well."

Humph. She was my age. Thirty. She'd freak if someone called her *ma'am*. But it also meant she hadn't recognized me. I touched my stomach. "Ate a rotter of a burger. Just need to find a loo."

"Oh." She pointed. "The portable toilets are over by the parking lot.

"Oh, right-o. Thanks, mate." I hustled off toward the parking lot, turned a corner, and ducked out of sight. I waited a few moments, then peeked out to see Daisy much farther along the row of vendors. Relief hit, and I took several deep breaths to steady my nerves. My disguise and British accent had worked.

The scent of grilled meat and onions wafted from a nearby hotdog cart, and my stomach grumbled with hunger. I bought a sausage on a bun, slathered it with mustard, and sat at a folding picnic table beside the cart.

I stayed alert for any familiar faces as I ate but soon got caught up in assessing personality types, which often happened, whether I wanted to or not.

After I left Shadow Falls, I wanted to figure out why I'd done what I'd done, so I took a course at the Rhys Thomas Institute on the five main types of personalities. Each type has easy-to-spot physical clues and a few common traits.

A funny thing about those traits—the same one can be a flaw on the dark side and a gift on the light side. It all depends on the degree of one's emotional wounding.

Then I learned more from Margaret Lynch Raniere about empowerment--how hiding our hated traits keeps us powerless. And what we need to do to ignite our inner power.

I popped the last bite of my sausage into my mouth just as a platinum blond family wandered up to the cart—a man and woman with four children.

Around eight years old, the middle two kids, twin boys with buzz cuts, all skinny legs and arms, pushed at each other.

Ah, Leader types in the making. If they grew up too entrenched in their dark side, they'd become aggressive, in-your-face rebels who'd blow up their lives. If they got enough positive attention and embraced all of who they were, they might become leaders with enough charisma to start a movement.

"I want a hotdog," yelled one of the twins.

The oldest girl hung back. Gangly and awkward, she wore her hair in a ponytail. Her eyes lacked the dancing light of her siblings.

The youngest, a girl around age four, threw her arms around the man's thigh. "Me, too, Daddy."

"Aren't you cute," said the hotdog vendor.

She giggled.

I flicked a look at the oldest girl, who stared at the vendor. A flash of hope sparked before her shoulders dropped, and she hunched in on herself. It had probably been years since strangers had looked at her and called her cute.

With the birth of each new baby, I suspected it had become harder for her, as the oldest, to get the attention she needed, and at ten, maybe eleven years old, her time in the spotlight had passed. Hopefully, she'd find the spotlight again one day and get the courage to step into it.

"Oh, my," I said to the older girl in my British accent. "What a lovely sweater you're wearing. It makes your beautiful blue eyes pop."

She gawked at me. It was always the eldest of many siblings who had those far-too-serious eyes. A moment later, her smile was warm enough to melt ice cream.

I offered the picnic table to the family, then wanting a reminder of something good I'd done, I moved back to capture the whole scene in a photo. I took it just as three women appeared. I checked the picture. Good, although visible, none of the women had blocked the oldest girl, who still beamed.

I wandered through row after row of stalls and saw a lot of new faces. The last time I'd searched the town's website, the population had grown from a hundred to a little over fourteen thousand people.

I rounded a corner and spotted the new owner of the café bakery, the one and only Marie Holinder. She'd set up a display of baked goods in her stall. Posted signs advertised sugar-free and gluten-free options. *Ack.*

Since one of my closest ex-friends hadn't recognized me in my disguise, I doubted Marie would. I edged closer.

Still slim and fit, Marie wore what she'd call dressy yet casual designer jeans with a silk blouse. Her strawberry blonde, straight hair fell to the middle of her back. Deep in conversation with a tall, rugged, blond man, she leaned into him and placed her hand on the mermaid tattoo on his left bicep. Her standard flirty move hadn't changed since high school.

He laughed at something she whispered in his ear. The familiar goofy look of a man about to cross the line appeared on his handsome face. Marie only targeted men in relationships—unless she'd changed in the past four years. I doubted it, which meant some woman was about to get her heart broken.

Hard to blame Marie, though, because the gorgeous man's grin promised roller-coaster fun.

Marie and I had been friends until she'd stolen my boyfriend in high school. Or I should say, he'd let her steal him.

I never figured out what I'd done to make Marie angry. One day she turned cold enough to get a part-time job as an ice sculpture, except around my boyfriend. With him, she burned hot as molten lava. His was the first goofy grin I'd seen, and after she'd hooked him, she dumped him. Marie had got her revenge on me.

A woman appeared beside the mermaid-tattooed man and touched his other arm in a he's-mine way. I took a closer look at him. Wow. An off-the-charts-hot, real-life Viking.

The woman said something and handed Marie a yellow postcard. I snapped a photo just as Marie smiled and took it. I moved my phone a fraction and snapped another picture, this one only of Marie. When I felt too homesick, I'd look at these pictures to remind me of the rotten things about Shadow Falls. Other than me.

My grip tightened on my phone as I scanned farther along the row of food vendors. Did Annie have a stall at the fair? A year after she'd lost out on the sale of the café bakery, she'd purchased an old diner and used the kitchen to start a catering business.

After she'd renovated the old place, she'd opened Annie's Diner and offered a high tea service in the afternoons. According to my grandmother, who raved about the food, customers traveled from nearby towns for Annie's afternoon tea service.

Marie turned to me when the woman and mermaid-tattooed Viking strolled away. "Would you like to buy a pie?"

I shook my head. "Cracked crumpets, I'm in a spot of trouble. Can't seem to locate me mate's stall. Keep getting lost in this maze. Annie Parker's her name." I might've just mashed upper-class English with another kind of British speak. Fortunately, Marie didn't notice.

"Annie's not here this year. Just as well. Her baked goods

lack a certain something." Marie gestured. "However, my apple pies—"

"Quite." What a witch. I pivoted and strode away.

I already had a baked gift to bring to tea. Hopefully, GG wasn't too sick to try one of my unique, homemade, melt-in-your-mouth tarts.

I checked my phone—almost teatime. And I'd risked being recognized long enough. Twelve minutes later, I'd driven up the escarpment, crossed the bridge over the Shadow River, and turned onto GG's quiet street.

My breath caught at the sight of the half-acre property dotted with oak trees, their buds starting to open. The two-story, three-bedroom house held so much more than just GG. The first time I'd finally felt safe again after the car accident. Sleep-overs with Annie. The back-porch swing where Jake first kissed me.

I parked in the wide driveway, retrieved my purse and home-made tarts then headed to the front door.

Long-ago images of Annie, Jake and me playing amongst the trees flooded me. I raced up the steps to the covered porch as if I could leave those memories huddled in the forts we'd built.

Two pots of yellow and purple pansies, one on each side of the front door, brightened the porch. I knocked, something I'd never done before. I ignored the pang in my heart and forced a smile.

GG flung open the door, and her face lit up as she held out her arms. "Olivia, you came. It does a body good to see you."

"I missed you, GG." Tears welled. Still holding the tin of homemade tarts, I hugged her gently to avoid crushing her possibly, sick gentle bones. Only she felt solid, with no smell of sickness, just the familiar, comforting smell of Chanel perfume. I stepped back, took off my sunglasses and eyeballed her.

For a sick seventy-year-old, she glowed with health. Her hair, now all white, was cut in a short, tousled bob with side-swept bangs. She wore stylish jeans, and her pink long-sleeved sweater enhanced the natural pink in her skin.

"Gorgeous Granny, you're not dying, are you?" I said.

She patted my cheek. "Not any time soon, darling. I love the blonde wig. Although..." She squinted at me. "Not sure I like how it changes your eyes."

Of course, she didn't. We shared the same smoke-blue eye color. "The reason why I chose this wig." The shade of blonde enhanced the blue but made the gray fade. "GG, are you even sick?"

"I had a terrible cold that turned into bronchitis." Her hand flew to her chest. "It sure felt like I was going to die. Come in."

I closed the door behind me. "GG, I'm glad you're not sick, but I took a chance coming here. If a cop had stopped me—"

"Don't you have fake I.D.?"

"No. I use my real name because extradition from one state to another is unlikely for my crime." I touched my wig. "Because you almost convinced me you were near death, I spent a hefty sum on this."

"I wanted to see you. And since I don't know where you live, I can't show up on your doorstep, so I had to get you here somehow."

I sighed and handed her the tarts. "For our tea."

"Thank you. Are you going to tell me where you live?"

I removed my coat and wig, placed them on a bench in the foyer then fluffed my curls. Ah, relief. "Boston."

"How can you afford the rent there? Are you living in a hovel?"

"I have a job and a roommate, although she might move to Chicago. She's there now for a job interview."

GG gasped. "Did you move in with a stranger?"

"No. We met at the three-year personality course I told you about. Then we took more courses together on the chakras. Oh, and a ten-day intensive in psychosomatics."

GG's face went blank. "Psycho what?"

"Psychosomatics. An in-depth way to read body language."

"Oh." GG hitched her head toward the living room and led the way. Just outside the open French doors to the room, she asked, "Is your roommate running from the law, too?"

"Yup. She's wanted in two states for multiple counts of murder."

GG stumbled to a halt as her face drained to a grayish-white. I put my arm around her shoulder. "Just teasing. Vivian's as legal as they come. She won't even jaywalk. And I'm a server now in a restaurant. All legal." Except for getting paid cash under the table.

GG clutched at her chest. "Don't scare a body like that."

"Sorry."

She smiled and patted my cheek again. "Now come and sit. I've got an offer I hope you can't refuse."

Chapter 2

I'VE GOT AN OFFER I hope you can't refuse. "What kind of offer?" I asked.

"Tea first."

I followed her into the living room. She'd moved her recliner kitty-corner to the couch facing the fireplace. The coffee table held the familiar blue porcelain teapot dotted with seagulls, matching cups and saucers beside a plate of finger sandwiches.

She opened the tin of tarts and stared at them. "What are they?"

"A Canadian treat called butter tarts. Try one."

She eyeballed them with skepticism as she picked one up and took a mouse-sized nibble. Her eyes widened. "Delicious." She took a bigger bite.

We sat on the couch in appreciative silence while each ate a buttery, sugary, flaky delight.

GG poured me a cup of tea. "Do you still take it clear, no sugar?"

"Yes, thanks. I'm curious. What's your offer?"

She sat back. "It took a lot of research on the World Wide Web, but—"

"Ah, Google Granny strikes again. First, no one calls it the World Wide Web anymore. And second, you can't believe everything you read online."

"I now understand why you veered off track from an honest, upstanding citizen to stealing the money."

So, she wanted to go there. The personality course hadn't shed much light on why I'd done what I'd done. Maybe GG had the answer. "What did you figure out?"

"You're angry."

My mind flipped back to that day Jake had gone M.I.A and I'd decided to take the money and run. A time of heartbreak, the fear of never-ending grief, but no anger. "At what?"

"Not at what. At whom."

No one came to mind. "Who am I allegedly angry at?"

She poured herself a cup of tea and added a dash of milk. "Jake O'Grady."

"I don't want to talk about him." The cup rattled on its saucer as my hand shook.

"Anger is one of the stages of grief," GG said. "And you never got angry. You need to rant. At the government for sending our troops to the Middle East. At the universe for how unfair it all is. And at Jake."

In the chakra courses, I learned about anger in the second chakra, and when anger gets buried, all kinds of nasty things happen. None of it applied to Jake and me. "I'm not angry. And if you mention Jake again, I will leave."

"I'll table it for now." She sipped her tea. "And stealing physical things is a metaphor for stealing love."

I'd have laughed in the past, but not after what I'd learned in courses some people called woo-woo. It never took me long to prove them wrong. "This sounds like it might involve Jake."

"And your parents."

Only forty when I was born, my widowed grandmother had claimed she was far too young to be called Grandma and had insisted on GG. She'd taken me in after a head-on collision had killed my parents. Five years old, I'd somehow survived the crash with no physical injuries. The accident and my parents' death were now a distant memory—most of the time.

My father was GG's son. From the day the drunk driver killed my parents, GG had refused to drink even alcohol-free wine. No spirits for her. She drowned her sorrows and celebrated her joys with tea. She raised her cup as if to give a toast. "You've lost too many people you love. Deep down, you don't believe you deserve it. The stealing—"

"Okay, Godfather Granny, please tell me about this offer you hope I can't refuse."

GG set her cup on its saucer. "Redemption."

I blinked. "What?"

"Redemption. Annie told me you paid her back."

"I paid her back double what I owed her." My voice filled with enough outrage to start a movement. "And she still refuses to talk to me."

"Even if you gave her ten times the amount you stole from her, it won't make a difference because she can't trust you."

I dropped my head in my hands. Annie had become my forever best friend since I'd shown up as the new kid on the first day of kindergarten. She'd sensed my emotional turmoil, beamed a smile as wide as the falls, wrapped her skinny little arms around me and said, *Don't be sad. I be your friend.* The formula for instant best friends when you're five years old. (Her grammar did improve.)

I raised my head. "She'll never trust me again, will she?"

"Maybe if you make it up to her in another way."

"How?"

"I'll get to that in a minute." GG leaned in. "I've done well in the stock market lately, so I want you to use some of my money and all the stuff you learned in Boston to help your friends. They need more from you than just getting back the money you stole. Move back to Shadow Falls and live with me. Reverse what you did."

Not what I'd expected. I sat back. "You keep telling me I'm not that person. But I am. I stole the money. Why do you want to do this for me?"

She picked up her tea cup, took a sip then returned the cup to its saucer. "Do you remember your first overnight Girl Scout camping trip?"

I shuddered. All that came to mind were the late night horror stories, often involving a crazed axe murderer waiting for one of us to step out of the tent. "What about it?"

"I gave you ten dollars to buy supplies for a merit badge."

Argh. A shameful memory I'd buried long ago. "Yes, I remember. No need to rehash it."

"I should've waited with you until the bus arrived." She sighed. "But you were ten years old, and five Scout Leaders were watching you girls. How you and your little friend managed to sneak away is beyond me."

It seemed Guilt-Trip Grannie wanted to rehash every detail. "Yes, I shouldn't have let Janet convince me to sneak away to buy candy with the ten dollars. And I get how it was like stealing ten dollars from you."

GG smiled as she leaned over the coffee table to pat my cheek. "That's not why I'm talking about the incident." She sat back. "Do you remember what you said when I asked you what your punishment should be?"

I drifted back to that time. "I suggested I give three months allowance to a homeless shelter."

"That's right. You saw your first homeless person at that bus station in Buffalo."

"I remember Janet and I each gave him two chocolate bars."

"And that's the person you are. Don't let that one theft four years ago define the rest of your life. I know you feel regret and remorse. And I want to see you happy again before I die." She straightened. "Better add Guru Granny to your arsenal of GG creations."

I cracked a smile. "Why?"

"Because there is only one path back to happiness for you, little grasshopper. Redemption."

I never expected a chance for redemption, mostly because I believed I didn't deserve it. A lightness filled my chest for the first time in years, only to leak out again. "I can't. The statute of limitations for my theft isn't over for another year. How about I move back then?"

GG didn't hesitate. "The offer is only available now. Redemption isn't supposed to be easy."

Staying away from the people and Shadow Falls was the hardest thing I did, even worse than exercise. But the possibility of prison... "I don't know. How else can I help them?"

"Marie's café bakery is booming because she offers sugar-free and gluten-free options, but she hasn't been able to create a tasty lemon meringue version. Annie has. She's hosting a drop-in event tonight at her diner to promote it. You can help her."

My grandmother reached for her purse, pulled out a white letter with a yellow scalloped border and handed it to me. It was a personal invitation for GG to attend the unveiling of Annie's new sugar and gluten-free lemon meringue baked goods.

"Well," I said, "if anyone can bake some delicious into the tasteless, it's Annie. I still don't understand how I can help her."

"Did you see the bottom of the invite?"

I read it out loud. *Enjoy a free tea leaf reading along with a tasty tart.* Okay, so?"

"Annie called earlier in a panic to ask if I knew a psychic because the one she hired canceled." GG gestured at me with her teacup. "How about you take her place?"

Time to add Goofy Granny to the list. "Uh, because I'm not psychic."

"Use the personality stuff and body language you learned in the psycho program you took."

"It's called psychosomatics."

GG set her teacup down. "Can't you use...what you just said and pretend to read tea leaves?"

I raised my eyebrows. "You want me to pretend to be a psychic? Dishonest, don't you think?"

Guru Granny wagged a finger at me. "If no one gets hurt, sometimes the end justifies a dishonest means. If you tell the truth about what you see in the people who want their tea leaves read—" she spread out her arms "—there's no harm done."

Hmmm. I had an excellent base to fake it as a psychic with what I'd learned. But I doubted Annie wanted my help. "I don't think so."

"She's paying two hundred dollars. And I've never heard her in such a panic. She's worried she'll lose her diner."

I desperately wanted to see Annie again to explain why I'd stolen from her. Except... "I bet she'd rather declare bankruptcy than allow me to help her."

"No one ever said redemption was easy. Do you want it?"

Even more, than I wanted Jake. My heart panged. Really? Not possible. Or was it?

I sat for a good minute, waiting for the intensity to lessen. It didn't. I wanted redemption. I wanted my friends to forgive me so I could forgive myself.

"Yes, I want redemption," I said. "Just not sure how to persuade Annie to let me help her tonight, though."

"Don't tell her it's you," GG said. "Go in your disguise."

I straightened. "That might work. I ran into Daisy today, and she didn't recognize me. I'll borrow one of your blouses in a color I'd never wear."

"Wait," GG said. "What about your voice?"

"I'll speak British. I've been practicing."

"British isn't a language. It's a nationality, and they speak English."

"Whatever, Grammar Granny." I grinned. "Call Annie and tell her you found a replacement psychic."

Chapter 3

A PROFESSIONAL SIGN ON Annie's diner window read *After-noon Tea Daily from 2:00 to 4:00 p.m.* A handwritten note taped to the front door read *Lemon Delight Event 7:00-9:00 p.m. By Invitation Only. (Staff, please come to the back).*

Three minutes late for the six-thirty staff meeting, I rounded the building to the propped-open back door and entered the kitchen where the scent of fresh-baked pie assaulted me—in a good way

Annie stood with three other women, presumably staff, by a stainless-steel table covered with lemon meringue tarts. She looked fabulous, wearing an emerald green blouse and a white skirt. Her beige blonde, she preferred honey-blonde, hair cut short into a mop of curls, suited her slim, oval face.

I missed my best friend as much as I missed Jake. Over the years, Annie and I had erupted into enough giggles to bottle it and sell it as laughing gas. And like any loyal friend, she had guarded my secrets as if they were hers.

I'd stupidly believed our friendship was unbreakable.

I blinked back tears. *Olivia, get your mind out of the if-only trap.* I shifted my focus to her staff.

Two wore yellow cotton dresses and white aprons. The third wore a short-sleeved white chef jacket with black pants. The three women looked familiar, especially the one with freckles, but I couldn't place them, maybe due to the hairnets they wore.

No one noticed me as I edged closer.

Annie waved at the two women in dresses. "Rose and Sarah, you take turns with half-hour shifts to collect invitations and names of people who want a tea leaf reading."

The freckled woman made a face. Her nametag read Rose. "What if *she* shows up?"

She? Ah, no doubt Annie's competitor, Marie Holinder.

The other server, Sarah, tsked. "Very inappropriate to show up without an invitation."

My internal personality assessor switched on. Sarah was an Achiever type. *Inappropriate*—one of their two favorite words. The other—*appropriate*. They sprinkled those words into conversations almost as often as others said *hi*. Sarah stood as stiff as the starch in her wrinkle-free white apron.

I'd never share a deep, dark secret with a strong Achiever type because many are far too judgmental. Yet, I'd hire one in a heartbeat to work for me—their ability to organize and create structure out of chaos bordered on the amazing.

Annie waved a finger. "Marie did not get an invitation, so don't let her in."

"She'll make a scene." Rose's statement ended with a wail. "Then what?"

A stocky woman in her mid-thirties, it seemed like Rose had a good chunk of the Team Player personality, which explained her agitation about confronting Marie.

An excellent move on Annie's part to hire a Team Player because they tended to bend backward to help customers. People pleasers on steroids—Team Players hated to cause conflict because it riddled them with guilt.

Annie bit her lip. Over the years, I'd watched her dancing around anger and never land on it. At the first hint of conflict, she'd joke, compliment or clam up. Whatever tactic worked at the moment. A few times, I'd seen her turn and run at a speed fast enough to put wind to shame.

A Creative type, she hated face-to-face conflict—not because she felt guilty—because she feared retaliation in some horrific way.

Maybe one reason why she'd never responded to me.

"Oh, you know Marie's going to show up," the woman in the chef jacket said. "And no matter how good your new tarts taste, she will slam them. And if she does, I'll slam her."

The chef's V-shaped body, fiery eyes, and the energy she emitted screamed the Leader type personality.

"No, Kirsten, you won't." Annie drummed her fingers on the table. "Did you throw out the rest of those leftover test tarts?"

"No." Kirsten grimaced. "Two yucky ones are in a plastic container at the back of the refrigerator. One is sugar-free, and the other is gluten-free. Do you want me to toss them?

"Not yet." Annie tilted her head and smiled her sneaky passive-aggressive smile. "If Marie shows up, she'll slam the tarts. So, let's not make a liar out of her. Let's serve her those yucky tarts."

Oh, Annie. Don't. Just tell her she's not welcome.

"Great idea, boss," Kirsten said. "I want to see her face when she eats one."

Rose and Sarah agreed. No surprise, Marie's popularity with women had not improved since I'd left town.

"Where are the samples for the people who'll arrive later?" Annie asked her chef.

"They're on a tray just inside the refrigerator."

Annie turned to her servers. "So, remember. Yucky tarts in a container at the back. Delicious tarts on a tray at the front."

Rose and Sarah nodded.

"Text me when Marie arrives, and I'll get her those two test tarts." Annie checked her watch. "I hope the new tea leaf reader gets here soon."

I lifted my chin to look down my nose. Very upper-class British. "Hello, there."

Everyone turned, and their eyebrows almost hit the top of their skulls—no doubt at my makeup.

Glamor Granny had decorated my face with baby blue eyeshadow, ruby red lips and a purple star on each cheek. She'd also found a pair of black-framed, tinted star-shaped glasses in her bag of costume accessories.

I looked beyond ridiculous, but I didn't care because I didn't look like me.

Someone suppressed a giggle.

"I'm..." My mind went blank. I'd tossed around some mystic-sounding names, starting with Madame, but never settled on one. "I'm here to read tea leaves. Nothing like a good cuppa, eh?"

Where were these words coming from? Not one of those YouTube clips showed British royals saying *cuppa* or *eh*.

"Oh, you're English." Annie strode to me.

I sucked in air. Now came the test of all tests. Would my best friend since kindergarten recognize me?

She stopped two feet from me and smiled. "Thank you for this. I so appreciate it. Come with me, and I'll show you to your table."

I'd deceived Annie again, and even though this time it was to help her, guilt still pooled in my belly as I followed her into the dining section. It looked nothing like I remembered.

A new industrial-size refrigerator covered half a wall. A long counter with glass-covered shelves below it ran almost the length of the diner. The fridge and the counter shelves were stocked full of lemon meringue pies.

Annie had replaced the linoleum floor with wide planks of hardwood polished to an almost blinding gleam.

She guided me past ten square tables to one tucked into the corner. A tented card on the table read *Tea Leaf Readings—For entertainment and amusement purposes only.*

"Oh, sorry, I'm in such a fluster, I didn't introduce myself or the others." She smiled. "I'm Annie Parker."

"I'm Madame, ah, Mystic."

"Madame Ah Mystic?"

"No, just Madame Mystic." I indicated the table with four chairs. "Is this where you want me to sit and read tea leaves?"

Annie stepped back and squinted. "Olivia?"

Bloody buckets of bones. I'd already forgotten to speak with a British accent. Perhaps I could distract her—often easy to do. I swept my arm in a panorama gesture. "Love the white scalloped cove ceiling. If you paint the walls yellow, you'll create a solid lemon meringue pie vibe."

"I can't believe Guileful Granny tricked me into hiring you."

My heart warmed. Maybe our friendship still had a chance. She'd just played the GG word game. "Ooh, good one. What does it mean?"

Annie pointed at the door. "Go. Now."

"Go Now Granny? How about Go-Go Granny? She's still got those boots from the 1960s."

Annie gritted her teeth. "*Guileful* means cunning. Now, please leave."

"Come on, Annie. You've stuffed down enough anger at me to fill an ocean liner. And all you can say is, please leave. You sound like a Canadian. Get mad. Yell at me."

"I'm not angry. No point. It doesn't change anything. And you're obviously still deceiving people. Now leave."

"I came here tonight to help you out of a jam. And you'll never forgive me if you don't let out your anger."

She gaped at me. "Forgive you?"

The door from the kitchen creaked open. Rose rolled a cart holding three empty three-tiered dessert trays and set them on one end of the counter.

"Please give me a chance to explain," I whispered.

"What's to explain?" Annie kept her voice low. "Because of

you, I didn't get to buy the café bakery I wanted."

I kept my eye on Rose as she placed a placard in front of each tiered dessert tray. The server didn't appear to be listening. "Let me stay," I whispered. "Otherwise, you won't have a tea leaf reader."

"You're not a psychic," she hissed.

"I've taken some courses on personality and psychosomatics. I can fake it. You advertised free tea leaf readings. Imagine what Marie Holinder will say when she finds out—"

"Okay, fine. You can stay, but only because I'm desperate." Annie pointed. "Sit there. Just give five-minute readings." She pivoted, walked a few yards, then rounded on me. "I am not paying you."

"Fair enough." She'd allowed me to stay. Yay. One tiny step toward forgiveness.

The server pushed the cart toward the kitchen.

"Annie, wait."

"What?"

By the time I got to her side, we were alone. "When our other friends show up, you'll keep my identity a secret, right?"

Annie harrumphed. "First of all, they are no longer your friends."

I ignored the jab to my heart that statement caused.

"Second," she continued, "they aren't coming tonight. I had a private showing the other night for close friends."

Another jab to the heart. I'd topped the list of Annie's close friends four years earlier. One mistake, okay, one colossal mistake later, I'd ruined a twenty-one-year-old relationship and lost my best friend.

I nodded and smiled, a smile I knew didn't reach my eyes. Annie didn't return the smile.

She and her staff set up the room for the next ten minutes.

Sarah, the rigid one, used one-half of the countertop for tea service. She placed an open wooden box of teas beside a tall silver hot water dispenser shaped like a giant teapot. Beside it, she stacked porcelain cups, saucers, a silver sugar bowl and a milk container.

Rose filled the tiered trays with lemon tarts. One tray for the gluten-free version. Ack. One tray for the sugar-free. Ack. And the last three-tiered tray for the sugar-free *and* gluten-free tarts. Triple ack.

Just before seven o'clock, Annie gave her staff a final pep talk. "Tonight, the tarts are just samples." She pointed to the industrial-size, glass-doored refrigerator. "Tell all the guests we've got the same version in a pie for sale. And if Marie shows up, remember to text me right away."

The servers nodded. Annie and her chef went to the kitchen.

"It's time." Sarah dragged a table close to the front door and removed her hairnet. Her dark brown hair fell into a shoulder-length bob, not a strand out of place. She unlocked the door, and several people shuffled inside before she sat at the table to collect invitations. More people lined up.

The first two guests, an older couple, tried a triple-ack tart, raved about it and bought four pies. They left without a tea leaf reading.

Next, a woman in her mid-forties tried a tart and signed up for a reading. Her waist looked tiny compared to her curvy hips. She had a good chunk of the Emotionalist type of personality. Clingy and weepy on a bad day, but on a good day, someone with a genius level of emotional intelligence.

She settled into the chair across from me and handed me her teacup. I examined the tea leaves for a few beats while I recalled traits of her personality type. I smiled as I mentally reminded myself to speak British. "You love animals."

She arched an eyebrow. "A lot of people do."

"Not everyone captures bugs in their homes and releases them outside."

She drew back in surprise. "How did you know? I don't tell people because they think I'm nuts."

I swayed as if in a trance. An itch popped up again on my left temple by the edge of the wig. "Because you feel so deeply, you wonder if you're an empath."

Her jaw dropped.

The itch worsened. Not very psychic-like to scratch. However, I could pretend to use my hand to decipher a message from a mystic spirit. Closing my eyes, I swayed and cupped my hand to use my fingernails to scratch the itch in a slow circular massage-type way. Ah, relief.

I blinked my eyes open to stare straight into the woman's large, dark brown ones. Like most Emotional types, they shone like pools of liquid. "I sense you can't hold back your tears. And it cheeses you off at times, doesn't it love?"

Her eyes welled up. "I'm such a suck. Do you know how I can stop?"

"I sense it's your superpower."

"No, it's not." She swiped at her eyes and scowled. "It's a curse. It's so embarrassing."

I stared into her teacup. "I see you don't feel discomfort when someone else is grief racked. You encourage people to feel what they feel, and you never ply them with trite expressions like, *everything happens for a reason*, or *time heals all wounds*."

She sniffled. "That's so unhelpful, not what they need when emotional."

"Exactly." I moved my hand to touch hers. "Because of your deep sensitivity, you allow your chums to feel what they feel. Like I said, your superpower. It's a gift."

The scowl slipped off her face, replaced with childlike wonder. She beamed at me. "I've never thought of it like that before. Thank you. I've gone to many psychics, and you will be the first I've ever recommended."

I ignored the ripple of guilt and smiled.

After she left, I had a steady stream of customers. In the five-minute time allotment, I "sensed" a couple of their good traits and touched on one shadow trait to explain how it was their superpower. Most of them asked me for a business card. I responded with, "Only in town for a brief visit."

At eight-forty, GG wandered over to me. "Everyone's impressed with you. The personality and psycho-stuff work."

"It's called psychosomatics."

"Oh, dear, you know I'll never remember. I came to say goodbye."

"Cheerio."

The crowd had thinned out, and I no longer had a lineup of clients. Annie appeared with two tarts on a plate. "Do you want a tart?"

Sugar-free. Gluten-free. Taste-free. "No, thanks. I'm not hungry."

"Come on."

"Oh, all right." I took the plate just as Sarah appeared. She smoothed her hands over her still wrinkle-free apron and whispered, "Marie is here."

Annie frowned. "You were supposed to stall her while you texted me."

"Rose told me that Marie has an *invitation*."

"What?" Annie whirled.

I looked toward the door. Marie spotted Annie and strode toward us.

"Do you want me to get the leftover test tarts for Marie?" Sarah whispered.

"No."

A flicker of disappointment rippled across the server's face.

Marie clicked her tongue. "Let me try one of your allegedly delicious lemon meringue tarts."

Come on, Annie. Tell her she's not welcome.

Annie smiled, reached over, took the plate of tarts from me and handed them to her competitor. "Here's a sugar-free one and a gluten-free one."

Marie picked up a tart, took a bite and swallowed. She grimaced. A hush fell over the room. The few people still left inched closer. Marie glanced at the small crowd, smirked and finished both tarts, her face contorting into various yuck expressions as she chewed and swallowed. "Your new tarts taste just awful."

"They do not," one woman said. A few others agreed.

Annie smiled, her sneaky smile.

My temple itched again.

Marie moaned and clutched her stomach. "I need to stop at the clinic on the way home." She stumbled to the front door and left.

"What a drama queen," Sarah muttered.

I waited for the small crowd to disperse before asking Annie the question I already knew the answer to. "Were those the test tarts?"

"Yes."

I blinked. "You gave them to me first."

She shrugged. "I didn't think Marie would show up. So wasteful to throw them out, don't you think?"

Such a typical Annie move, and it hurt as much as if she'd slapped me across the face. "Still the sneak queen of passive-aggressive, I see. Are we even now?"

"Never. We're done."

My breath hitched. Forget redemption. If Annie, the biggest-hearted person I'd ever met, couldn't forgive me, no one would. But I refused to let her see how much I hurt. "What, no thank-you for tonight? People raved about me."

"If I see you again, I'll call the sheriff."

I left before she saw the tears flooding my cheeks.

The next day, the sheriff called GG's house looking for me.

Chapter 4

GOURMET GRANNY MADE BREAKFAST while I swiped through the pictures I'd taken the day before at the fair. I paused at the one with the platinum-blond family. My heart warmed at the sight of the beaming oldest girl. About to swipe to the next photo, the three women who'd stepped into the picture just as I'd snapped it jumped out at me.

Annie's chef and two servers.

No wonder they'd seemed familiar. Kirsten had left her hairnet on the evening before. The picture showed the chef had shoulder-length hair, darker than Sarah's chestnut color. Rose, her red hair tied in a ponytail, had her head flung back laughing, the camera catching the light in her eyes.

Something about the picture niggled at me, but I let it go when GG deposited a plate of bacon, eggs and hash browns in front of me. I put my phone down and picked up a slice of bacon. "You left too early last night." Between bites, I told her about Marie's dramatics.

GG rolled her eyes. "She often makes nasty remarks about Annie's baked goods. No one will believe her now because everyone thought Annie's tarts were delicious."

I also told my grandmother about my decision to return to Boston. "Even though I already paid Annie back, she said she'd call the sheriff if she sees me again."

GG shook her head. "I doubt it." She picked up a piece of toast and smothered it with her homemade blueberry jam. "What about your other friends? Did you ever pay them back?"

"I will. Money's tight, so a little at a time."

"If you live here, I'll give you access to all...um, some of my money."

I wavered until I remembered Annie's last words to me. No way I'd stay in Shadow Falls without her friendship. "I promise I'll come to visit you once a month."

"Stay," GG said. "I thought you wanted redemption."

"I do, but I'll have to find it some other way."

My grandmother's landline rang. She picked up the old-fashioned ivory wall phone on the third ring. "Good morning." She paused to listen. "How awful. And so young. How did she die?" GG's eyes bugged open. "A suspicious death?"

My grandmother and her friends claimed they were far too young when someone their age died, and maybe the police should check for foul play.

"Of course, I won't tell anyone." GG hung up and hurried back to the table. "Remember, my friend Nancy, the nurse?"

"Yes, I've only been gone for four years. Is she still working at the hospital?"

"Yes. That was her on the phone. Marie Holinder is dead."

"What? How?"

"Not sure. It's a suspicious death because someone called the police. Fudge nuggets. Nancy had to hang up because a patient rang for her. She said she'd call me back."

The landline rang again, and GG picked up on the second ring. "Hello." She paused. "Oh, Sheriff, what can I do for you?"

GG looked at me, her forehead pleated. "Yes, she's still here."

I gasped. Annie had ratted me out to the sheriff—time to hoof it out of Shadow Falls. I raced up the stairs to my old bedroom. Panic clawed at my throat as I threw clothes into my suitcase. I'd paid Annie back, so her charge might not hold up in court. But the other seven women I'd stolen from, no doubt they wanted me behind bars.

A minute later, GG appeared at the door. "Olivia, stop. Trevor wants *Madame Mystic* to meet him at Annie's diner."

I let out a sigh of relief. The sheriff hadn't asked for Olivia Twist. "Did he say why?"

"To answer some questions about the event at Annie's Diner last night."

"What kind of questions?"

GG shrugged. "I don't know."

I'd known Trevor Wilson in grade school. A sarcastic kid, we'd found him amusing, but the teachers hadn't. "Did he sound sarcastic when he said Madame Mystic?"

"No, he sounded dead serious."

"Since Madame Mystic has only appeared at Annie's event last night, I bet this has to do with Marie's death."

"When he tells you about it, act surprised," GG said.

"Don't worry. I won't rat out my Gossip Granny, who promised Nurse Nancy she wouldn't tell anyone."

GG rolled her eyes. "Get dressed. I'll get the eye shadow and lipstick. Is there any chance Trevor will recognize you?"

"Not even without my disguise. He moved away before high school."

"Just in case, remember to speak with your British accent."

Forty-two minutes later, I arrived at Annie's Diner. The front door was locked. I peeked through the glass. Annie and the sheriff stood by the counter. Both stepped toward the door when I knocked, but Trevor stopped Annie to unlock the door himself.

"Thank you for coming, Madame Mystic," my ex-best friend called out, her tone laced with friendliness.

I detected slight stress on my new name. Whew. My real identity could hide under my wig, for now.

The sheriff held open the door and eyeballed my outfit without indicating what he thought of it.

Trevor Wilson looked good in his dark blue uniform with a brass star on each collar and his sheriff's badge pinned above the left pocket. He still had a thick head of blond hair, but he'd shot up and grown into a handsome man around six inches taller than my five-foot-five.

Annie stepped forward and stopped just behind him. As big as kiwis, her green eyes twitched with an unreadable message. She held up two fingers and mouthed some words. They might as well have been in Russian.

"Come in," the sheriff said.

I gazed at him through my star-shaped glasses and remembered my British accent. "Delighted to make your acquaintance, Sheriff. May I ask what this is about?"

"I need to ask you some questions." He whirled toward Annie. "Don't speak until I say so."

Wow. What had she done to upset him? This setup felt off. If he wanted my version of the events without Annie's input, why question me in her presence?

GG had emailed me when Trevor became sheriff. One of her friends, the maintenance man at the sheriff's office, had said Trevor often spouted off theories based on flimsy facts but always found solid evidence before he made an arrest.

He gestured to a table. "Please sit."

Annie smiled at me. "Madame Mystic, would you like coffee and a slice of pie?"

My stomach growled. I'd abandoned my breakfast to get here. "Yes, mate. How delightful. I'm a bit peckish." Drat. I might've just mixed a British accent with an Australian one.

She hurried away while I settled into a chair.

Trevor sat and crossed his arms. "Annie tells me she hired you as the tea leaf reader for last night's event."

"Yes, and what a delightful event."

He narrowed his eyes a fraction. "Did she pay you?"

I blinked. Something in his tone told me how I answered mattered. "I don't often work for free."

My non-answer might buy me some thinking time. I recalled what GG had said. *She's paying two hundred dollars.* Ah, Annie's two-fingered message became clear.

"What about last night?" the sheriff asked. "Did Annie pay you?"

"She most certainly did. Two hundred dollars."

"Huh. Are you aware that fortune-telling is a misdemeanor in New York state and subject to jail time and a fine?"

I did not. Fortunately, I remembered the tented card Annie had placed on the table and took a stab at bluffing. "Even if it's clearly stated it's for entertainment and amusement purposes only?"

He harrumphed. "Why did Rose tell me she heard Annie say she wouldn't pay you?"

I plastered on a fake frown. "Golly, Sheriff, I don't know."

The redhead had walked into the room when Annie had told me to leave the night before. What else had she heard? "What else did Rose say?"

"She said the two of you argued about something."

"Most peculiar because we didn't argue."

"Yeah, Annie said the same." The sheriff rubbed his chin. "And neither Sarah nor Kirsten saw any tension between you two. I wonder what got Rose so confused?"

"I can't say because I don't know her."

Annie appeared with a tray of two coffees and two slices of lemon meringue pie.

The sheriff eyed the pie as if it might bite him. "Annie, please put that down, sit at another table, and keep quiet."

She slid a pleading glance my way as she set the pie and coffee in front of the sheriff and me. Too bad, I had no idea what her glance meant.

She placed the empty tray on another table. As she pulled back a chair, someone rapped on the door.

"Tell them you'll be closed for the next few hours," Trevor said.

Annie unlocked the door, and a woman in a deputy's uniform stepped inside. She looked like a younger Hallie Berry when she'd worn her hair short. The deputy strode to the sheriff and whispered in his ear.

"Good," he said. "She'll call me direct?"

The deputy nodded and pulled a folded paper from a back pocket. "Here's the search warrant."

Uh-oh. What were they looking for?

The sheriff took the paper and handed it to Annie. "We've got a warrant to search your premises."

My old friend straightened her shoulders. "I've got nothing to hide."

Trevor faced his deputy. "Jayla, I'll join you when I'm finished here."

"I'll start in the back." She swiveled and strode into the kitchen.

Annie's hand shook as she read the warrant. I reached up and patted her arm. "Please do tell. What dastardly event has occurred?"

She looked at the sheriff.

He answered me. "Just before dawn, Marie Holinder died."

"Oh, crikey, how positively horrid."

He drilled me with a steely gaze. "The coroner suspects poison."

Annie tossed the warrant on the table and fisted her hips. "And because of Marie's reaction to my lemon meringue tarts last night, the sheriff thinks I poisoned her."

Chapter 5

My mouth fell open. Sure, Annie had a passive-aggressive streak broader than the Shadow River, but murder? No way—even if murder by poison was a sneaky passive-aggressive way to kill someone.

"What kind of poison?" I asked.

The sheriff hesitated for a beat. "Based on the smell, the coroner has a suspicion. She's running tests. And Annie, no one's accused you yet."

"Does Annie need a lawyer?" I asked.

"No," she answered. "I've done nothing wrong."

Trevor pointed at the chair beside mine. "Sit there and keep quiet."

She sat.

In cop shows, sometimes they separated people for questioning, and sometimes they didn't.

The sheriff cut his gaze between Annie and me as if searching for an answer to a question he hadn't yet asked.

I put my arm around her shoulder. "Annie a murderer? Absurd. Utterly absurd."

"Maybe. I've known Annie since grade school. How long

have you known her?"

"I told you," Annie said. "Meg Twist recommended her to me yesterday when the other tea leaf reader canceled."

Scowling, he rounded on her. "And I told you to keep quiet."

Again, I wondered why he allowed Annie to stay while interrogating me, especially since she ignored his do-not-talk orders.

He thrust his chin at me. "Is this true? You only met last night?"

"Quite true. I arrived yesterday for a visit. I heard Annie was in a spot of trouble and needed a psychic."

"Yet you claim she's not a murderer. Absurd," he mocked me, "utterly absurd."

"Because, Sheriff, I can read people. I am a psychic."

"I don't believe in psychics."

"Am I just a figment of your imagination then?"

He harrumphed again.

I took a bite of pie. "Mm. Annie, how criminally delicious."

She froze. The sheriff squinted at me.

Drat. Wrong choice of words. "Perhaps your chef made this."

"No," Trevor said. "Annie's pie recipes are a secret. Only she knows the ingredients."

"Oh." I put down my fork and threw her an I'm-sorry glance.

The sheriff pushed his untouched plate to the side. "Please describe the events of last evening from the time you arrived."

"I arrived a few minutes late for the staff meeting. No one noticed me at first."

He shot a look at my outfit. "Really? Why not?"

"They were having a right old natter."

"What about?"

The words echoed. *Text me when Marie arrives, and I'll get her those test tarts.* The ones Marie had eaten.

"Oh, nothing much, just some particulars for the event."

"What exactly did you hear?"

No way Annie poisoned Marie, but if I told the sheriff everything, he might use it as ammunition against her. I told him what I'd heard, except for the conversation about the test tarts.

Trevor sipped on his coffee. "Anything else?"

"I don't think so."

"You didn't hear some talk about giving Marie test tarts?"

Cracked crumpets. Wow, I'd just thought in British. It happens when you become fluent in another language.

"Well?" the sheriff demanded.

"I'm attempting to recall the conversation."

Of course, he'd find out. Five of us were there. "I do believe I heard some banter about test tarts. Sorry, old chap. I forgot."

The sheriff set his coffee cup down. "You forgot?"

"Yes. You see, we don't eat test tarts in the UK. I'm not sure what they are. We've got other tarts. Apple tarts and—"

"Annie," the sheriff interrupted me. "Tell Madame Mystic exactly what you told me about your test tarts."

She bobbed her head. "I had to experiment with different types and combinations of sweeteners and gluten-free flours. Some of those test tarts tasted just awful."

The sheriff drilled her with a beady gaze. "Easy to hide a poisonous substance in an already nasty-tasting tart."

"I told you—"

"Enough," Trevor said.

She clamped her lips together and threw me yet another glance I couldn't decipher.

"Any test tart leftovers?" I asked.

The sheriff nodded. "Two. Annie threw them out."

"Then why don't you jolly well retrieve them from the rubbish and get them analyzed? I'd wager you won't find any poison in them."

"Garbage got picked up this morning," Annie said.

"Very convenient for you." The sheriff swung his gaze to me. "Now you know what American test tarts are."

"Right-o."

And I now suspected why Trevor wanted Annie and me together—to gauge our reactions to each other's comments.

"Go on," he said to me, "what happened next?"

Smack in the middle of a verbal minefield, I trodded with care as I described the events of the night before. As I got closer to the part when Annie showed up at my table with the plate of test tarts, she stiffened beside me. There was something she didn't want me to say. But what?

"Oh, dear." I placed my hand on my chest. "How utterly embarrassing, old chap, but I must use the loo."

What I needed was some think time.

Trevor's phone rang. He glanced at the display. "Go ahead, but hurry."

I sauntered down the hallway to the women's restroom, entered and locked the door. What had Annie told the sheriff?

Drat her passive-aggressive ways. I recalled fragments of conversation about those stupid test tarts as I paced.

Did you throw out the rest of those leftover test tarts? Annie had asked her chef.

No, Kirsten had replied. *Two yucky ones are in a container at the back of the refrigerator. One is sugar-free, and the other one is gluten-free. They're in a plastic container at the back of the refrigerator. Do you want me to toss them?*

Not yet, Annie had answered. *If Marie shows up, she'll slam the tarts. So, let's not make a liar out of her. Let's serve her those yucky tarts.*

I stumbled to a halt in front of the sink. Trevor had said Annie had thrown out the two leftover test tarts.

Not true. Marie had eaten them. Not realizing Annie had given me the test tarts first, the staff would've told the sheriff there were two left. And Annie had played along, said she'd thrown them out.

Therefore, she must've lied to the sheriff and told him she'd brought me two good-tasting tarts, both of which Marie had eaten.

But why lie? Any of her staff could've switched the test tarts for poisoned ones. Ah, but none of the others would've given me the test tarts set aside for Marie.

When Marie had shown up, Sarah had whispered to Annie, *Do you want me to get the leftover test tarts to give to Marie?*

Annie had said no because she had just given them to me.

No wonder Annie had lied to the sheriff about what tarts she'd given me. She'd denied the friction between us and made it a point to tell Trevor we'd only just met. If Annie admitted she'd handed me the test tarts on purpose, she'd need to explain why she'd given horrible-tasting ones to a perfect stranger.

Warmth spread through me. Annie wanted to keep me out of jail.

My turn to keep her out of jail. Only Annie and I knew the test tarts were on the plate she'd given me. This explained the desperate attempts at nonverbal communication she'd thrown my way.

Undoubtedly, the sheriff wanted to see if I'd corroborate whatever Annie had told him.

When I returned to the front of the diner, Trevor stood and gestured for me to follow him to the table where I'd sat to read tea leaves the night before.

Annie followed us. "Don't speak," he ordered her. "If you say one word, I will arrest you."

Then why let her stay?

Annie went pale enough to warrant a blood transfusion.

Ah. The sheriff wanted to watch her reactions to what I said. She'd never had a poker face, and no doubt, he'd picked up on that. I threw her an encouraging smile.

"Exactly where were you when Marie ate the tarts?" he asked.

I pointed at the chair tucked into the corner. "There."

"Please sit there and describe to me what happened."

"Right-o." I moved behind the table and sat. "Toward the end of the event, Annie brought me a couple of her tarts."

"Did you see her plate these tarts?"

"No. Before I took a bite, Marie appeared and asked to taste an allegedly delicious tart."

I smiled up at the sheriff. "Then Annie reached over, retrieved the plate she'd given me and gave it to Marie."

I described Marie's reaction to the tarts she'd eaten and her parting words about the clinic. I felt a pang of regret. We'd all thought she'd faked her dramatics to humiliate Annie, but perhaps the poison had already started to affect Marie.

"So, as you can see, Sheriff, it's absolute rubbish that Annie poisoned Marie because she gave those tarts to me first."

"Unless she also planned to poison you."

No wonder Annie had kept my real identity a secret. If that got out, he'd think she'd planned a twofer murder. I'd known Annie all my life, and she wasn't capable of murder. Someone else had switched those test tarts with poisoned ones.

I hopped to my feet. "Ridiculous. We've just met, Sheriff. What's her motive to off me?"

Trevor hooked his thumbs into his belt. "I don't know. But it does beg the question, who was the intended victim? Madame Mystic or Marie Holinder?"

I gaped at him—bloody buckets of bones (wow, still thinking in British). I'd be dead, if I'd eaten the sugar-free and gluten-free but not poison-free tarts.

"What's your real name?" Trevor asked.

I staggered back a step at yet another blow. "I prefer you call me Madame Mystic."

He removed a pen and paper from his front shirt pocket. "Give me your real name and address."

I blinked. If I gave a fake name, he'd soon find out. And if I hesitated for too long, he'd not believe me. I sent a silent apology to my Boston roommate. "Vivian Quick. My address—"

"Oh, Sheriff," Jayla called out. "I found something."

The lilt in her voice meant she'd scored something significant.

She held up a tattered, emerald green, soft-covered book. "You're going to want to see this."

Oh, crikey.

Annie whimpered.

Chapter 6

I HELD MY BREATH. The deputy waved the green book as she strode toward us.

Annie's journal. Its contents might land us both in jail.

"Did you find the bottle?" the sheriff asked.

Bottle of what? I glanced at Annie, stiff and white as a mummy.

"Uh-huh," Jayla said. "Bagged it for forensics. You've got to see this book. It's a journal. Sort of."

If only Annie journaled like your average person who rambled on about daily events, the sheriff would get bored two paragraphs in.

But no, Annie called her book *My Wishing You Bad Karma Journal*. No rambles, just a list. A list of people who'd hurt, shamed or angered her—no doubt they'd find my name in her journal.

After she wrote the culprit's name, she'd place her right hand on the page and chant—*I wish you bad karma. I wish you bad karma. I wish you bad karma.* Then she'd wait. Not for an opportunity to express her feelings. She'd wait for some outside force to cause the person some grief. All because she froze when confronted with face-to-face conflict.

I'd thought Annie's bad karma list odd for years because she's the gentlest of women. I recently learned two things about anger. Everyone gets angry, even those who claim they don't. And buried anger always comes out somehow, even through the tip of a pen.

She'd started the wish-you-bad-karma list in high school. At first, she'd listed the culprits on a piece of paper she kept folded in her purse until I'd given her the journal.

The deputy handed Sheriff Trevor the book. He opened it and read my inscription out loud. "Happy graduation to my BFF. May all your dreams come true. Love, Olivia."

Big, bold letters etched in silver on the front cover read, *Create your dreams. Do what you love. Follow your heart.* She'd flipped open the book and had stared down at the blank-lined pages for a good minute, perplexed.

I'd suggested she use it to write out a long-range plan. She'd looked as pained as if I'd asked her to put a shredded manuscript back together. Then her eyes lit up, and she'd said, *This is now my wishing-you-bad-karma journal.*

"I'd forgotten about Olivia Twist," Trevor said.

I jerked my head when the sheriff made that pronouncement. Fortunately, he and the deputy didn't notice because they were looking at Annie.

She snapped out of her mummified state and reached for the journal. "That's private property. It's personal."

The sheriff pulled his arm back. "The search warrant says otherwise. Is Olivia still in town?"

Didn't Trevor know what I'd done? It seemed not. I eased my shoulders down slowly and took a deep breath.

Annie shook her head. "Olivia moved a few years ago. I don't know where."

"Olivia Twist." Jayla pursed her lips. "Like a female version of Oliver Twist?"

"Her father loved Charles Dickens books," Annie explained.

Trevor's forehead pleated. "If I remember correctly, her parents died in a car crash a long time ago."

Annie nodded.

"Sad," Jayla said.

"Yes, very." Annie held out her hand. "Please give me my book back."

Trevor flipped a page and scanned it. Eyes wide, he stared at Annie. She visibly swallowed.

"What is this?" he asked.

She blinked. "It's my journal. When I get mad at people, I write down their names and wait for something bad to happen to them."

He squinted at her. "Just wait?"

"Yes. After something bad happens, I cross their name off the list."

The sheriff read more. "I see you record what happened to them."

"Yes," she whispered.

How many names had she crossed off? And how many, like mine, still needed a visit from karma? I now realized that a journal topped the list of bad gift ideas for a passive-aggressive.

"Why don't you write down what they did to get on your list?" Trevor asked.

"Because I never forget."

My mouth dried up as Trevor flipped and scanned through more pages. No doubt he'd find Marie's name.

"Lots of names here," he said. "You've got Greg Wilson. Fell off the bridge and almost drowned." The sheriff directed a beady gaze at Annie. "Greg still claims someone who knew he never learned to swim snuck up behind him and pushed him off the bridge. Lucky for him, a nearby boater saw him fall. Did you push Greg off the bridge?"

"Of course not."

"What did he do to get on your list?"

Oh, Annie. Why didn't you just tell Greg off at the time?

"He dumped me in our senior year on Valentine's day."

"Creep," Jayla muttered.

The sheriff shot his deputy a look. When she gave a whatever shrug, I decided I liked her even though she'd outed Annie with the journal.

"Here's Olivia Twist's name." His eyebrows drew together in a half frown. "I thought you said she'd moved away."

"She did."

"But you wrote here, killed by spitting cobra in Africa."

My head snapped toward her. She dropped her gaze to the gleaming wood floor.

Jayla gasped. "What a horrible way to die."

Yes, it was. Annie had wished for me one of my deepest fears. The reason I'd never visit Africa, not after I'd read about the spitting cobras. From up to twenty feet away, they could blind their prey by spitting venom at their eyes. After that, they'd slither over and squish them to death.

My actions had ripped Annie to her core, and that knowledge killed me more than any spitting cobra might've. (Okay, maybe not.)

Annie focused on her clogged feet. "Olivia didn't get killed in Africa. She moved away."

Trevor frowned. "Why did you write this then?"

"Sometimes, I get caught up in a revenge fantasy and write it down."

Her words from the night before popped up. *I'm not angry. No point. It doesn't change anything.* Right. No buried anger there.

"What did Olivia Twist do to you?" Trevor asked.

Goosebumps covered my arms. I pushed up my glasses and calculated my best escape route out of the diner. And out of Shadow Falls because this was Annie's chance for payback.

Instead, she shook her head. "Olivia did nothing, not really. It just hurt more because we were best friends since kindergarten."

Her words stabbed at my heart. An image of Jake appeared.

The time he told me he'd enlisted. Had I hurt Annie as much as he'd hurt me? I shook it off—no time to delve into that.

If she told the sheriff I'd stolen money from her, and he discovered the real identity of Madame Mystic, he might think she'd intended to poison me. Marie's death had Annie all muddled up. A quick investigation and he'd find out what Olivia Twist had done. He'd wonder why Annie had downplayed the theft.

Yet, if she told him, some of the anger she claimed she didn't feel toward me might dissipate. I couldn't fix everything, but this might help her.

Swaying, I closed my eyes. "Annie, I sense this Olivia woman did something most appalling to you." I widened my eyes. "Oh, my. You've tried to bury the severity of her actions to lessen the pain."

Ignoring Annie's glare, I used my right palm to make a circular motion in front of her chest. "Your heart chakra is stricken with grief. I see it in your aura."

Her glare sharpened as if I'd just morphed into some crazy, rambling woo-woo.

Jayla stared at me with fascination. "My aunt claims she can read people's auras, too."

The sheriff cleared his throat.

I continued. "Oh, crikey. I sense a deep betrayal. Olivia Twist betrayed you."

"Did she steal your man?" Jayla asked.

My old friend's jaw tensed, and she threw up her arms. "Olivia stole seven thousand dollars from me."

"When?" Trevor asked.

"Four years ago. She skipped town and before you ask, I don't know where she is. And it's not a big deal anymore, because she paid me back."

Humph. She failed to mention I paid her back twice what I owed her. But then again, she'd lost the café bakery because of me.

"Did you report it?" Jayla asked.

"No."

Stunned, I momentarily dropped my mystic demeanor to gape. I'd assumed all my friends had reported the thefts.

"Why not?" Trevor asked.

"I just told you. Olivia paid me back."

But at the time, Annie didn't know I'd pay her back. I thought the sheriff might pick up on that. He went a different route, instead. "If she skipped town, how did she pay you back?"

"Online money transfers."

Once again, the skin on my left temple by the edge of my wig itched. I swayed again, cupped my hand and used my fingernails to scratch it in a slow circular massage-like motion. "I sense there's more to the story."

Annie threw me a desperate, shut-your-yap glare.

Of course, if I pushed her to tell the whole story, the sheriff might conclude she had a double motive for poisoning Marie. The murdered woman had belittled Annie's baking and ended up with the café bakery my best friend had wanted.

"Oh, blimey, I've just interrupted you, Sheriff. I apologize." I waved at him. "Do continue."

He lifted the journal. "Will I find Marie Holinder's name in here?"

Annie's eyes grew as big as limes. Her face got even paler. "Maybe."

Jayla snorted. "That woman goes around town trash-talking your baked goods, and *maybe* you've put her name on your list. I'd put her on my list. If I had a list." She grinned. "Maybe I'll start a bad karma list for wanted criminals. Save the taxpayers some money. What do you think, Sheriff?"

"Let's just focus on this crime." Trevor opened the journal and continued to scan pages and mutter names. He stiffened and handed the book to Jayla.

He reached for his handcuffs. "Annie Parker, you're under arrest for the murder of Marie Holinder. You have the right to remain silent. Anything you say can and will be used against you in a court of law…"

Chapter 7

THE NEXT MORNING AFTER breakfast, I cleaned up while GG called her friend, the maintenance man at the sheriff's office, to get information about Annie. She listened for a good minute before she said, "Thanks, Marvin. My lips are sealed."

Gossip Granny hung up and let out a low whistle. "Annie's bail is five hundred thousand dollars."

"There's no way she murdered Marie."

"The sheriff thinks he has irrefutable evidence."

"What evidence?"

"Marvin doesn't know yet and said he'll snoop around."

I scrubbed at a plate like the dried egg residue was a murder charge. "The sheriff arrested her when he saw Marie's name in the journal. I've got to help Annie through this mess."

"She just got transferred to the county jail and can't afford to put up the money for bail."

"What about her parents?"

"I don't think they can help her. Not enough collateral."

I whirled. Soapsuds flew onto the floor. "You need to post Annie's bail."

"I don't need to do any such thing. Finish cleaning up, make me a fresh pot of tea, and let's talk."

Curses. GG planned to bribe me, just like she did in high school when I wanted the pink satin prom dress with the flared skirt and sweetheart neckline. All I had to do was mow our enormous lawn while the guy who usually cut it was sick. He didn't get better until the end of July.

Ten minutes later, I set GG's blue teapot on a hot plate on the kitchen table, scuffed back a chair and sat. "Let me guess. You'll put up Annie's bail if I move home."

GG smiled—such an angelic smile. She often used it to disguise the devil in her. She poured us both a cup of tea and added milk to her cup. "You can direct me on how to use my money only if you move back to Shadow Falls and live with me."

She held up her hand. "Before you say yes, understand you must pay back and help each of the friends you robbed in a non-monetary way."

"I didn't set out to rob them."

"I know. Do you agree to my terms?"

I took a sip of tea. "You won't pay Annie's bail unless I agree."

She smiled her angelic smile again.

Wear the itchy blonde wig, garish makeup and kooky outfits for another year until the statute of limitations had passed? The clock above the microwave ticked while we sipped our tea. I'd need to stay incognito for a year, but it wasn't often one got redemption handed to them with a cup of tea. The clincher—Annie might just forgive me.

"Okay, devil woman." I smiled. "I agree to your terms."

"Generous Granny is a more accurate name."

GG set out in her siren-red Chevy Tahoe while I showered and dressed in my Madame Mystic disguise. I'd just finished applying layers of makeup when GG called to tell me she'd finished posting bail. "If you leave now, you can get there in time to pick up Annie."

I drove forty miles outside town to the county jailhouse and waited for Annie beside my car. Minutes later, she walked out with flattened hair, wrinkled clothes and dark circles under her eyes. "Why are you here? And don't you own another outfit?"

"You're wearing the same clothes as yesterday."

She cracked a smile. "You didn't spend the night in jail."

"I posted your bail. Do you need a ride home?"

"To the diner. My purse is there. And don't you mean Generous Granny posted my bail?"

Déjà vu. I smiled at the reference to GG. "Technically, I did."

Annie tilted her head and eyeballed me. "How? Another robbery spree?"

I ignore her jab. She deserved a few. "Redemption."

"What?"

"Redemption. It means—"

"I know what it means. What do you mean?"

Another déjà vu. Just what I'd said to GG. I waved at the passenger side door of the car. "Get in, and I'll tell you."

"I'll listen because you bailed me out. Thank you."

"What's it like in jail?" I asked as we settled into our seats.

"The guards were nice. Some scary inmates." She slammed her door shut. Her nostrils flared. "Something you should've experienced."

Something I never wanted to experience. I Ignoring the sting of her comment, I cranked the ignition. No push-button start in the old Echo.

"My phone is in my purse," Annie said. "Can I borrow yours?"

She called the diner and talked to her chef about a few upcoming events while I veered onto the county road that led to Shadow Falls. We were close to town before she said, "Bye, Kirsten. Oh, please call Rose and Sarah to tell them I'm out of jail."

Annie hung up. "So, what's this redemption thing?"

I outlined GG's offer. "That's why I showed up at your event last night. To help you out."

Before she could tell me what I'd done didn't come close to

redemption, I rushed on. "I get that we're not square yet, but what do you think about GG's offer?"

She tilted her head. "Not so sure they'll forgive you, even if you pay them back twice what you stole and help them in a non-monetary way."

"I don't mean something like spring clean their house." I gripped the steering wheel harder. "I'll find a way to change their lives for the better. And until the statute of limitations is up, I've decided to reveal my identity only to you."

She snorted. "Reveal?" She snorted. "I figured it out."

I smacked the steering wheel. "Because I forgot to speak British. That won't happen again."

"British isn't a language. The British speak English."

Wow, a triple déjà vu morning. "Now you sound like Grammar Granny."

Annie cracked a smile. A sign she'd thawed somewhat toward me.

I pulled up to a red light. "Your chef is at the diner. Let's go to the falls for some privacy and figure out who had the means, motive and opportunity to poison Marie."

Annie's lips curled into a sneer. "Look who's switched to the right side of the law."

Sometimes the magnitude of what I'd done made me want to crawl into a hole somewhere in a forest and die. But if I let the shame swamp me or let Annie's anger continue to get in the way of our investigation, she'd end up in prison for a murder she didn't commit. "Maybe we should hash out what happened between us first."

She crossed her arms. "No."

Time to dish out some Madame Mystic wisdom. I took a deep breath and rolled down the window to let in some fresh air. No automatic windows in the old Echo. "I know conflict is hard for you, but the passive-aggressive way you deal with anger, it's not healthy."

"Why not? It's served me so far."

Annie often lived in some delusional otherworld. "What about the mess you've gotten yourself into now?"

"What do you mean? It's not my fault."

Of course, she'd think that.

A horn blasted behind us. The light had turned green. I stepped on the gas, and the Echo chugged forward. "Why didn't you fight back when Marie belittled you?"

"Olivia, you know I'm not one of those people who gets all aggressive and attacks people even after they've attacked me."

True. It wasn't Annie's nature. Even if she had it in her, I didn't want to push her to become someone who got all in your face, belligerent and aggressive.

I pulled the car over to the curb then turned to face her. "You act like your only other option is to retreat. Doesn't it feel sucky always to retreat?"

My conflict-avoiding friend rolled down the passenger window and sucked in fresh air before she turned to me. "Yeah. But what else can I do?"

"With Marie, you could've called her on it, not in an aggressive way, but—" I flicked my wrist "—a stand-your-ground way. Instead, you secretly wrote her name down on a bad karma list, secretly wrote down your revenge fantasy and secretly gave her yucky tasting tarts. All of which resulted in a charge for her murder."

"I see what you mean," Annie reluctantly agreed. "But I can't deal with what you did to me and this murder charge at the same time." She gestured at the road. "Stop idling. It causes pollution."

I stepped on the gas, sighed and switched mental gears. "Okay, we'll talk about it after we figure out who murdered Marie."

Annie's eyebrows flew up. "What?"

"Do you think the sheriff will look for other suspects?"

Her brow wrinkled, and she rubbed her eyes. "No."

"Then, we need to investigate."

She gaped at me.

"I want to help you find the real killer, not just for redemption." I stepped on the gas and veered back onto the road. "You didn't kill anyone."

Silence.

I glanced sideways. "Did you?"

"Of course not. How do you propose we do this?"

I pulled up to another red light. "We ask questions, find evidence of the real killer and bring it to the sheriff."

She threw me a genuine smile that lit up her eyes. "Do you really think we can?"

"Yes. GG told me the sheriff thinks he's got irrefutable evidence against you. So, we've got to find out what it is and blow it wide open."

Her eyes dimmed. "Do you remember when Trevor got the call yesterday when you asked to go to the loo?"

"Yeah."

"It was the coroner. She called to report the poison that killed Marie was pure lemon oil."

"Furniture polish?"

"Yes. Deadly when swallowed. And..." Annie's voice trailed off.

Dread snaked up my spine. "Drop your bombshell before the light turns green."

"Four years ago, after Marie got the bakery, she gloated about it, right out loud, to my face, every time she saw me. I wrote her name in my journal, just her name."

Annie let out a long sigh. "Then later, every time I saw her, she bad-mouthed my lemon meringue pies, and my mind leaped into a revenge fantasy. It's amazing how often they pop up."

I sucked in air. "Annie, what did you write beside her name?"

"Died from lemon oil poison."

Chapter 8

DIED FROM LEMON OIL poisoning—what were the odds? The light turned green as my mind raced with the implications of this news. Once through the intersection, I pulled my car to the curb again. "Before Jayla found your journal, only the murderer would've known Marie died from lemon oil poison."

"Sheriff Trevor thinks I poisoned Marie and wrote it down."

"Fried frackle, what made you choose lemon oil poison as your revenge fantasy?"

"Is that your new non-curse word?"

In our teens, when another friend had cursed in front of GG, she'd blasted him, then later told Annie and me that cursing was unacceptable, but it was okay to occasionally use a non-curse word to show displeasure.

"Uh-huh, what do you think?"

"I like cracked crickets better. Anyway, back to your question. I bought some pure lemon oil to clean the diner's floor before my event."

"When did you buy the lemon oil?"

"Last week. It works like magic. Doesn't the wood gleam?"

"Just like your eyes when you wear emerald green." (A genuine compliment never hurts when seeking redemption).

Annie threw me a brief smile. "I got the idea because my pies and the furniture polish share the same word. Lemon."

And she just had to write it down. I stepped on the gas and eased onto the road. "This isn't good."

"Nope."

"Someone found your journal, saw what you wrote and framed you for the murder."

"I figured that out last night."

Our pool of suspects could fit into a hot tub, and my friend had hired them.

I turned into the public lot beside the park. We climbed out of the car and meandered toward the falls. Dark clouds threatened rain. Only a few diehards, mostly fitness buffs and dog walkers, were out and about.

I pocketed my key. "Do you think one of your staff killed Marie?"

A pained expression settled on Annie's face. "Yeah."

Without words, we crossed the lot toward the beach.

I drew in a big breath. "On the night of the event, when you talked about giving Marie test tarts—"

"I set up the perfect opportunity for one of them to switch out the real test tarts with the poisoned ones. Instead of Lemon Delight, I should've called it the Lemon Deadly event."

Annie had a habit of joking during tense situations. It annoyed some people.

We giggled like little girls. For a heartbeat, it felt like the good old days, back when she didn't hate me.

"Annie Parker," a nearby woman called out.

Mrs. Briggs, wearing an orange velour tracksuit, bore down on us. One of our high-school teachers, she'd reveled in giving detentions. A group of us tried to keep track of the number of times she'd said, *shame on you*, but we'd lost count.

Just in time, I remembered not to greet her.

"Hello, Mrs. Briggs," Annie said.

Our old homeroom teacher's wrinkles deepened as she frowned. She'd thickened over the years, and with her gray hair cut short enough to see her scalp, she looked like a bulldog—not a cute one.

She lifted her chin. "I must say, Annie Parker, if I'd known you'd turn out a murderess, I'd have given you more detentions."

I'd forgotten just how fast juicy news spread in Shadow Falls.

Stupefied, Annie stared for a few beats before she hunched in on herself and swiveled her head as if to look for others who might also accuse her. It didn't take a psychic to figure out Annie had not expected people to believe she'd murdered Marie.

Using my right hand, palm forward, I drew air circles in front of Mrs. Brigg's chest. "I sense you were one of Annie's teachers."

She threw me a mocking look. "You sensed it?"

"I'm a psychic."

"How mystic of you after I mentioned detentions."

I dropped my hand. "Annie didn't kill anyone. So why don't you put a cork in it and sod off."

"What a rude psychic you are."

As Olivia Twist, I'd never have said what I just did to an old teacher. I smiled. Wearing my Madame Mystic disguise had at least one awesome perk. "And shame on you for condemning Annie before you're privy to all the facts."

Mrs. Briggs's mouth dropped open.

"Go on." I shooed her. "Get out of here with your tosh rubbish."

She huffed and strode away.

"I can't believe it," Annie whispered. "People think I'm guilty."

"Just idiots like Mrs. Briggs." I gave Annie a quick shoulder squeeze. "Let's go figure out who did kill Marie."

We fell silent to maneuver our way down a steep bank to the beach. Very few people around. A runner in tights whizzed by us, then pivoted, jogged up to me and ran on the spot. "Are you Madame Mystic?"

"Indeed, I am." Sheesh, I sounded pompous.

"You read my mother's tea leaves the other night. She raved about you, and I'd like to book a session with you. Do you have a business card?"

Hmmm. She wasn't the first to ask me, which gave me an idea—I could earn money as a psychic. "Not on me. I'll drop some off at Annie's Diner next week."

Still running on the spot, the woman frowned. "Is the diner still open after the owner poisoned the bakery lady?"

My friend stiffened.

"Annie Parker did not poison anyone," I said.

The woman jogged back a few steps. "If you say so. I'll pick up one of your cards next week." She waved and ran off.

"See," Annie said, her voice filled with hopelessness, "everyone thinks I'm guilty."

"Just two people who don't know you."

"I guess. How are we going to prove I'm innocent?"

I linked my arm through hers and pulled her forward. "First, we gather facts. Do you know if any of your staff hated Marie?"

"All of them hated her. My chef, Kirsten Olson, used to work at the café bakery until Marie yelled at her and publicly fired her."

"Yikes. With Kirsten's aggressive nature, she might kill for revenge over a public humiliation."

"I thought Kirsten liked me." Annie unlinked her arm and waved her hand. "I thought all three liked me. How delusional am I? One hates me enough to frame me."

"Not because they hate you. Because they hated Marie and saw the perfect opportunity, but maybe it's a coincidence. Don't you keep your journal hidden?"

"In my safe. After I bought the lemon oil and saw the big poison sign on the label, I dug out my journal and added the poison bit beside Marie's name. Then I got a call from a new client and threw it in a desk drawer. I forgot about it. That's where Jayla found it."

"Do all your staff have access to your office?"

"Yes, I keep extra supplies in there."

"What about a supplier or someone else?"

Annie shook her head. "I don't meet with anyone else in my office. It's too small."

"Then one of your staff found the journal and used your revenge fantasy to commit murder." I groaned and kicked at a big stick on the beach. "This looks bad, Annie, but I know you didn't do this."

Her eyes shimmered with tears. "Thank you for believing in me. I'm sorry I killed you off with a spitting cobra."

The apology meant another layer of anger toward me had thawed. My forever best friend might forgive me yet.

I retrieved the stick I'd just kicked and heaved it into the water. "Quite an impressive revenge fantasy. It made me realize you're right."

"About what?"

"You're not angry at me. You're filled with murderous rage."

She tilted her head. It was a typical move for the Creative type because it disconnected them from their bodies. They loved to space out and live in their heads to avoid unpleasant feelings in their bodies. "Maybe," she said.

Honestly. Death by spitting cobra—no murderous rage there. Since Annie refused to hash it out now, I just shook my head and led the way down the beach to our favorite log, a long, thick trunk of an oak tree, the bark ravaged by weather. Situated far enough away from the falls, we could hear each other talk and not get sprayed by the cascading water.

I gazed up to the top of the fifty-foot falls. Sometimes on sunny days, a rainbow appeared. We decided long ago that wonderful things happen after seeing a rainbow over the falls.

"We won't see a rainbow today," Annie said.

"Not with these clouds. Have you called your parents yet?"

"No. If I call them, they'll drive home from Florida."

I whistled. "Your mom will be furious you didn't call."

"I don't want them to cut their stay short. When they're gone, I feel like a mature adult instead of a loser thirty-year-old still living with her parents."

"I'm moving back in with GG. We can be losers together. Did you get a lawyer?"

"A court-appointed one, right out of law school." She picked up a rock and flung it into the lake. "He thinks I'm guilty and said he'd try to get me a plea deal."

"Cracked crumpets. What a useless wanker of a twit."

"Crumpets? Ah, the non-curse Brit version. I like it, but you don't need to speak British when it's just me."

"I thought British wasn't a language," I said.

"Whatever."

I smiled, then got serious. "Let's reason this out from the beginning. We'll start with, you being an excellent baker, and there's another reason why Marie ridiculed your pies. What did you do to her?"

Chapter 9

ANNIE KICKED AT THE sand. "I didn't do anything to Marie, but for some reason, she hated me."

"Why? There's nothing to hate about you."

"Now that's a true story."

I laughed. "Maybe it's because you're a better baker."

"I'm not."

"Then why do you think Marie was angry at you?"

Annie shrugged. "I've got no idea."

"Anger's a funny thing." My mind flipped through all the years we'd known Marie. "High school."

"What about it?"

I hopped to my feet. A few nearby seagulls took flight as I paced. "Sometimes, when people get angry at something, they think it's stupid to get angry about. Or they shouldn't get angry. Or they're afraid to express it. So, they bury the anger. And it often comes out directed at something else."

"Okay, I get that. What does it have to do with high school?"

"Marie spent the last two years of high school going after boyfriends of girls who made her mad. She succeeded every time."

I plunked down on the log close to Annie and bumped her shoulder with mine. "Except with Greg, who remained faithful to you."

"Until five months later, when he dumped me for...let's see if I can remember...oh, right. *No one*."

Yikes. Still a sore spot. Better get her mind back to something less painful, like her murder charge.

"Whatever Marie got mad at you about in high school, she never got her revenge."

"That was fourteen years ago, although Sarah can't seem to let it go."

Huh? "Sarah can't let go of how Marie tried to steal Greg from you?"

Annie flicked an annoyed glance at me. "No. She can't let go of how Marie stole her boyfriend back then."

What? My brain stalled for a beat. "Sarah went to high school with us?"

"Yeah, don't you remember her?"

"No."

"Think of her with mousy brown hair. She dyes it that beautiful cocoa color now."

I stared into the cascading water of the falls and tried to conjure an image of a younger Sarah with mousy brown hair. "No memory of her. What's her last name?"

"Miller."

I picked up a stick and wrote her name in the sand. "Sarah Miller. Was she the one always buried in a book?"

"Yes."

"Great." I nudged Annie with my elbow. "The I've-got-a-motive-to-kill-Marie list just got longer."

"I don't think so. Sarah's engaged to the man of her dreams."

"Didn't you just say she can't let the high school thing go?"

"Yeah." Annie frowned. "I wonder why because she's super happy now."

"When anger gets buried, it doesn't get buried dead. And

sometimes deeply buried anger can explode out of someone in a way they never thought possible."

I paused for dramatic effect. "Like with murder."

A seagull cawed.

"It did break her heart when her boyfriend dumped her. She canceled my tutoring sessions for a month. She's never forgotten it. Any chance she gets, she'll gossip about Marie."

Annie shivered and rubbed her arms. "And come to think of it, Marie acted okay toward me until a few weeks ago. Why wait fourteen years to go bitter on me?"

"After you bought the diner and offered the most delicious baked goods for sale, you became her competitor. And her anger at you about the original incident bubbled up."

Annie straightened. "Did you hear that?"

"What?"

She stood and peered into the bushes behind the log. "A meow. I heard a meow."

"Meow." It came from behind us.

"I hear it, too." I swung my legs over the log, stood and scanned the ground covered with twigs and shriveled old leaves from autumns gone by.

Huddled under a small bush was a three or four-month-old gray and white kitten. I pointed. "Over there. It's a kitten."

We approached slowly. "Don't be scared, kitty," I said. "Look at those blue eyes and gigantic ears."

"OMG," Annie said. "Something has scared the hair right off it."

"No." I picked it up. "It's a hairless, well, almost hairless cat. Wow, soft as velvet."

She touched its forehead. "And adorable. How did you get here, cutie?"

The kitten meowed back an unintelligible answer.

"Maybe, it's feral, and maybe there's more of them."

I cuddled the kitten while we spent the next few minutes searching the brush, careful where we stepped but found no signs of other kittens or a mother cat. The kitten purred as I massaged one of its gigantic ears. "We can't leave it here."

I dropped Annie off at home to shower and change while the kitten and I went to buy supplies. By the time I returned to get Annie, I'd fallen in love with the little gray and white cutie. "Wonder what GG will think about keeping the kitten," I said as I parked in her driveway.

"She'll love it," Annie said.

GG became Grumpy Granny the second she caught sight of the almost hairless kitten. "Olivia Twist, you find that rat-like creature a new home. It obviously won't shed, but look at those claws. It'll ruin my new furniture and drag kitty litter through the house, which means hauling out the vacuum..." Her complaint litany didn't stop as she walked into the living room.

"I'm revising my earlier comment," Annie whispered. "She'll grow to love it, just like when you brought home that hamster."

"Maybe I'll wait until then before getting this cutie a playmate."

Annie nodded in agreement. "Let's feed this little guy. Or gal."

We hurried to the kitchen, where I opened a can of salmon-flavored cat food. As the kitten gobbled down the food, GG strolled into the kitchen. "Olivia, we are not keeping that kitten."

Before I could respond, the landline rang. GG picked it up. "Hello." She smiled. "Sorry, you've got the wrong number. There's no Vivian Quick here."

Uh-oh. I snatched the receiver and hung it up. "Who was that?"

"Some young man." GG scowled. "Why did you hang up?"

"I panicked. When the sheriff asked me for my real name yesterday, I told him it was Vivian Quick."

"Oh, no," GG moaned.

"What's the big deal?" Annie asked. "Isn't that the alias you use?"

"No, she's my roommate."

"Why did you use her name?" Annie smacked my arm. "Why didn't you just make up one?"

The phone rang again.

Chapter 10

WE ALL STARED AT the ringing phone. If the sheriff had wanted to speak to me, why hadn't he identified himself to GG? On the third ring, I said, "Let it go to voicemail."

"No." GG reached for the receiver. "What if it's a friend in trouble?"

I snatched it from her hand again and didn't hang up this time. "Top of the morning to you."

"That's Irish," GG whispered.

"And it's past noon," Annie quickly added.

"Who is this?" A young man asked.

"Oh, blimey, don't you know who you're calling?"

The man cleared his throat. "Is Vivian Quick there?"

"That's me, old chap. Who are you?"

"I'm a new deputy with the sheriff's office. He wants your permanent address."

I gave him my Boston address.

"Thank you," he said. "Why did Mrs. Twist say I had the wrong number and then hang up on me?"

"What do you expect from an old woman who lives alone and gets the collywobbles when strange blokes call and don't identify themselves?"

GG turned into Glaring Granny.

"Sorry," the man mumbled.

"Don't worry. I won't mention it to the sheriff. Cheerio." I hung up.

"I'm not an old woman who gets the colly-whatever," GG said.

"Sorry, I had to come up with some explanation for the hang-up."

Annie threw up her arms. "Why didn't you just use a fake name and give a fake address?"

"Because I plan on living here." I paced around the kitchen. "If I'd given the sheriff a fake name, he'd have soon figured it out. When he searches my Boston address, he'll find everything connected to it—the internet, cable, electric—in Vivian Quick's name. I give her cash for half the rent. And I work for cash as a server."

"On television, the police always check social media," GG said.

I shook my head. "Vivian's a private person. She's not on social media. Neither am I anymore."

"Ooh," Annie said, "it's like Olivia Twist doesn't exist."

"You might tell a body," Glaring Granny said.

"Sorry, I meant to." I grimaced. "Vivian will freak out when she discovers I used her name as a fake psychic. She has a hate-on for psychics like no one I've ever met. Thinks they're all crooks."

"Only the one I know," Annie muttered.

Another jab I ignored. "Vivian's in Chicago for a job interview, so I won't tell her yet." I gnawed my lower lip. "Maybe never. We both use burner phones, so the sheriff can't call her."

"I get why you use a burner, but why does Vivian?" Annie asked.

"Said she prefers them. She's very secretive about her past. Enough about her. Let's go."

After the kitten had curled under a blanket on its new cat bed, we hopped in my car to drive to the diner.

"We've covered why Kirsten and Sarah didn't like Marie," I said. "What about Rose? What's her last name?"

"Flowers."

"Rose Flowers? Are you kidding me?"

Annie laughed. "No."

"Wow."

"Yeah. Anyway, Marie acted like she and Rose were comrades in red."

"Huh?"

"Marie had strawberry in her blonde hair. She often gave Rose skincare and fashion advice in a nasty way."

I darted a glance at Annie. "Like what?"

"Watch out for the squirrel," she yelled.

I jerked my gaze toward the windshield and slammed on the brakes. The squirrel stopped and darted back the way he'd come. "Whew." I stepped on the gas. "What kind of stuff did Marie say to Rose?"

"Stuff like, 'Oh, my, I stopped wearing that hideous mustard color years ago.'"

"Yikes. Mustard is a hideous color."

"You know that's true."

"So," I mused, "Marie also humiliated Rose. All three of your staff had at least some degree of motive. Are you sure no one else knows the ingredients to those lemon meringue tarts?"

"They know the ingredients, but only I know the exact measurements. And there's one secret ingredient no one knows about."

"Lemon oil?"

Annie inhaled sharply, and I slid a sideways glance at her. No smile, not even a crack. "Ah, too soon. Sorry."

"I keep the recipe a secret in case any of my staff quit and divulge it."

"Wait." I pulled to the side of the road, then twisted to face her. "What does it matter if anyone else knew the ingredients?

Those were test tarts. Someone made a batch of poison tarts and substituted them with yours."

"They were my test tarts. I could tell by the look of the crust. Keep driving. I told Kirsten I'd help her prepare sandwiches this afternoon for an event tonight."

My mind churned as I drove over the bridge and down the main strip. Who had laced those tarts with poison? And how?

I parked behind the diner, and we walked into the kitchen through the back door. No delicious aromas assaulted me this time. Alongside a cutting board, chef knife and vegetables, six empty baked pie shells sat lined up on the stainless-steel counter.

The chef stood by a small desk in the left kitchen corner, staring at the telephone receiver in her hand.

Annie made a beeline to the desk, scooped up her purse then hugged it to her chest. She smiled until she looked at her chef. "Kirsten, why aren't you preparing sandwiches for Mrs. O'Grady's function?"

Jake's mother. For some reason, the universe felt it necessary to hurl my ex in my face at every opportunity.

"She canceled fifteen minutes ago." Kirsten raised the telephone receiver. "Just got the fourth cancelation. There are no catering events for the rest of the week now."

Annie dropped her purse, staggered and grabbed the counter edge. "Oh, no. Everyone thinks I did it."

Sure, it made sense that Mrs. Briggs, who'd thought everyone guilty of something in high school, had assumed Annie had done it. But all these other people?

I picked up Annie's purse and set it on the desk. "I'm sure not everyone—"

"I don't believe you poisoned anyone." Kirsten paused for a few beats. "Unfortunately, some people do. Idiots."

"What did Mrs. O'Grady say?"

Kirsten's gaze dropped to the floor. "She said, 'Too bad someone didn't smother Marie's nasty self to death. Because now I can't trust Annie's food, can I?'"

Wow. No one seemed upset about Marie's death. Our list of murder suspects might very well extend beyond Annie's staff, except that only they had access to the inner workings of the diner.

Annie threw her head into her hands. "I'm ruined."

I put my arm around her shoulder and gave her a quick squeeze. "Only wankers think you're guilty." Time to act like a Brit who thought tea fixed all things wrong. "Fancy a cuppa, Annie?"

"If it's wine."

"Ah, yes, the American way. Do you have some here?"

She flicked a wrist. "Maybe, later."

Kirsten moved to the counter, picked up the knife, then chopped the bottoms off a celery bunch with one deft movement. "If business slows, are you going to fire me?"

"No," Anne wailed. "I'll need someone to run the place while I'm in prison."

For a second, a flash of relief flashed on Kirsten's face. I couldn't blame her for not wanting to lose her job.

If Annie went to prison for first-degree murder, she'd be an old lady before she got out. My heart sank. I shook my head. No. She'd not go to prison for a murder she didn't commit—not on my watch.

I eyeballed Kirsten and how deftly she handled the knife. Despite what Annie believed, how hard could it be for a chef to imitate someone else's tart shells? Not hard at all.

Sometimes an offensive move throws people off and tricks them into saying something they wish they hadn't or something incriminating.

I strode to the other side of the counter, out of knife reach and stood in front of Kirsten. "So, you don't want to get sacked and go on the dole? Maybe you should've considered that before you offed Marie Holinder."

The chef's mouth dropped open. "What?"

I jerked my right arm upward in full Madame Mystic mode.

Palm forward, I moved my hand in a circular motion. "I see violent thoughts dancing in your aura. You hated Marie Holinder, didn't you?"

Kirsten snorted and stabbed at the celery. "Of course, I hated her. Who didn't?"

I dropped my hand. "Why did *you* hate Marie?"

"Because I used to work for her. She humiliated people, cruelly pointing out any mistake anyone ever made in front of others." The chef leaned over the vegetables and locked eyes with mine. "When Marie fired me a year ago, I didn't try to kill her. I called her a horrible witch. Right to her face. Talk about satisfaction."

Kirsten smiled as she drew back. "Not long ago, I ran into Marie at the movie theater. I thanked her for firing me because I now worked for someone who wasn't a snarly hag. I told her Annie was the best boss ever."

Maybe Marie's recent attack on Annie's baking had nothing to do with some long-ago high-school incident. "When did this happen?" I asked.

"A few weeks ago."

Annie and I exchanged glances. She raised her eyebrows. She, too, had pieced together the reason for Marie's recent bitter remarks, who'd no doubt felt humiliated by the chef's outburst at the theater.

"It's a pleasure to work for you." Kirsten smiled at her boss. "I'd never do anything to jeopardize that."

Annie blushed and bobbed her head.

Kirsten rounded on me, raised her right arm and imitated my circular hand motion. "Tell your spirit guides they're barking up the wrong cloud."

"It happens. Other than the two of you, who else bakes?"

"No one," Annie said.

"Not like us." The chef grabbed the knife and cut several celery stalks into shorter sticks. "Although Sarah wants to learn to bake."

"Are you sure?" I asked. "Because someone did a jolly good job creating a good imitation tart."

Kirsten gestured at the baked pie shells with the knife. "See how these are empty?"

"Of course. I get visions, not hallucinations."

"Hold on." The knife clattered on the counter. Kirsten strode to the industrial-size refrigerator, yanked open the stainless-steel door then disappeared into the cold. Seconds later, she returned with a large glass bowl filled with a lemon pudding-like substance. She put the bowl on the counter.

"Annie made this lemon filling and—" she gestured at the six empty pie shells "—these crusts yesterday morning before the stupid sheriff hauled her off to jail. So, Madame Mystic, what can you divine from this?"

"Crikey." I faced my friend. "After you prepared the lemon filling for the testing, did you make the tarts right away?"

"No, I never do. I made three types of fillings with different combos of sweeteners, which sat in the fridge overnight."

"And the tart shells? Also, the day before?"

"Yup. I made up three trays of different types of gluten-free pastry. For one set, I used coconut flour and—"

I raised my hand. "So, to be spot-on clear. Everyone on your staff had access to the lemon fillings and the tart shells before you put them together and baked them?"

"Yes, but—"

"That, my mate, is what they call opportunity. And we've also got the means. Lemon oil poison. All we need now is a motive."

Kirsten crossed her arms. "Are you talking about means, motive and opportunity, like they talk about in cop shows?"

"Right-o," I said.

She glanced at Annie, then turned her squinted eyes back to me. "You didn't just get a psychic vision about me. You're trying to solve Marie's murder."

I jabbed an index finger at the air between us. "I did get a psychic vision." I lowered my arm and flicked my wrist. "However, at times, the mystic world is as hard to interpret as a thick cockney accent. And yes, I want to help Annie."

"Why get involved? You just met her the other night."

Uh-oh. Why indeed. My mind spun. I touched my left temple with my fingertips. "The mystic world mostly sends symbols a psychic must decipher, but the spirits are clear about this." I changed my tone to a ghostly sound. "Heeeellllp, Annie. Heeel-lllp, Annie."

Kirsten rolled her eyes so far back her irises disappeared.

"Very insistent," I said, in my normal British accent. "One hulky spirit guy is the leader of the pack. He's appeared before in my visions. Quite handsome, but at times frightful."

"Do you believe this garbage?" the chef asked her boss.

"Right now, I'll take any help I can get." Annie's forehead pleated. "I just remembered that we used all the lemon fillings the next day to make the test tarts. The four of us spent the day taste-testing. And we're all still alive."

Huh. Then how did the poison get into those test tarts?

Chapter 11

THERE WERE TWO OTHER possible explanations why Annie and her staff had all survived the taste testing. "Perchance, did you make more test tarts later?" I asked.

"No, I didn't," Annie said.

It had to be the other explanation. One I'd use to promote my reputation as Madame Mystic while dealing with my pesky left temple itch. Using my fingertips, I scratched the itch in a circular motion. "I'm getting a vision. Someone is sneaking into the refrigerator—"

"Really," Kirsten drawled. "Who?"

"I don't know. Very shadowy. Means it's nighttime."

"The light goes on in the refrigerator when you open it," Kirsten said.

"Not in my vision. Yes, it's the night before the taste testing. She's holding—"

"If the figure is so shadowy, how do you know it's a she?"

I wanted to tell Kirsten in a clipped British accent to sod off, but instead, I smiled. "I surmised because no men work here. We'll never get anywhere if you keep hating on the mystic world. To save time, let's assume I'm right."

"Fine. What's this shadowy woman holding?"

"A small bowl and some kind of a scoop with a handle."

Annie opened a drawer and pulled out two scoops. "Like these?"

"Yes. What size do you use for filling the tarts?"

"Why don't you ask the handsome, hulky spirit guy?" the chef asked.

"Okay, Kirsten," Annie said. "We get you don't believe Madame Mystic, but she's trying to help me."

"Sorry," Kirsten said, without any pretense of meaning it.

Annie placed a blue-handled scoop on the counter. "We use this number sixteen scoop."

I dipped it into the lemon filling and withdrew a level scoop. With my other hand, I tipped the bowl until the contents leveled. "This filling has settled. It appears none is missing. Someone scooped out enough filling, maybe little bits from each bowl, then later added lemon oil to it."

"Then stole two of my prebaked empty shells and made poisoned tarts." Annie's face brightened. "Great. We can prove someone else other than me had means and opportunity."

"Utterly peachy," I said. "Now, we just need to establish a motive."

We fell silent. Who had a strong enough motive to kill Marie?

The back door opened with a squeak.

Kirsten whirled, and her elbow knocked my hand. Lemon filling flew out of the scoop, and a glob landed on my chest. Some spattered onto my star-shaped glasses, so I removed them.

Annie's two wait staff, wearing clean white running shoes and yellow uniforms, entered the kitchen then stumbled to a halt when they spotted me.

Rose beamed a warm smile. "Hello, Madame Mystic."

"Cheerio."

"Oh, are you leaving?" she asked.

Mentally thanking Google Granny, I said, "Most Americans believe *cheerio* only means farewell. Us Brits sometimes use it as a greeting or a toast."

Sarah eyeballed my outfit and frowned with disapproval. "You're wearing the same thing you wore to Lemon Delight night."

"Yes, indeed I am." *You judgmental cow.* "Other than this glob on my chest." I thrust my chin at her. "As are you."

"This is my uniform."

Annie cleared her throat and handed me a clean cloth. I wiped the pudding off my blouse.

"You look familiar," Sarah said to me.

Uh-oh. I hadn't remembered Sarah from high school, but it appeared she remembered me. "Oh, ducky, remember we met the other night?"

She squinted. "No. You look like someone I know."

I forced myself to use the cloth and clean my glasses instead of jamming them on my face. Sarah had not thought she recognized me until she'd seen me without my tinted glasses. Note to self. Always keep glasses on, even if covered with pudding. I put them back on.

"For some reason," Sarah mused, "high school comes to mind."

"Went to high school in Boston." I swept my arm toward Annie. "Your boss is out of jail."

Rose flung her arms around Annie. "I'm so happy you made bail."

"Me, too." Sarah smiled but stayed put. The rigid types often avoided social hugging.

All three of Annie's staff seemed to like her. Yet, one of them had framed her for Marie's murder.

Rose grabbed a white apron and tied it around her waist. "I sure hope the sheriff finds the real killer soon."

Her type felt guilty when they displeased someone. If angered, they rarely expressed it. They stewed in resentment, the perfect catalyst for passive-aggressive behavior, and the Team Player's preferred way to deal with anger.

"What about you, Rose? Did you hate Marie enough to off her?" I asked.

Gasps echoed around the kitchen.

"How rude," Sarah said.

Rose's mouth dropped open as she paled, causing her freckles to stand out. She stepped back until she bumped up against the freezer door. "A lot of people hated Marie."

Even though I knew why Rose hated Marie, I wanted to watch her while she told me. "Why did you?"

"Because..." She swallowed. "Marie always made snide remarks about my clothes and my looks." Rose raised her hands and touched her flushed cheeks. "Stuff like, 'Oh, Rose, you might want to get rid of those hideous freckles. I've heard lemon juice works.'"

The L-word again. Lemon.

I turned to Annie. "Who cleaned the wooden floors with the lemon oil for the event? And when?"

"Rose and Sarah. Two days before."

"So, what?" Sarah said. "That doesn't prove anything."

Perhaps no one had read Annie's journal. Maybe Rose got triggered when she saw the word *lemon* on the bottle. Maybe still filled with resentment over the remark about the hideous freckles and lemon juice, she'd decided to bump her passive-aggressive behavior to the level of a sneaky murderer. And if so, maybe I could flush out the guilt.

"How utterly horrid of her," I said. "Bet you resented those comments."

"Sure, who wouldn't? That doesn't mean I poisoned her." Rose opened a bread bin, removed a loaf and tossed it on the counter.

Unfortunately, no sign of a guilty breakdown.

Sarah fisted her hips. "Why are you here accusing and questioning us about the murder?"

Kirsten, busy peeling an onion, chimed in. "Because her spirit guide told her to help Annie figure out who really poisoned

Marie."

"Seriously?" Sarah said, her back straighter than the planks in the diner's new wood floor.

I'd already pegged her as primarily the Achiever type. But like everyone else, they had a built-in rebel, often buried deep in the shadows of their psyche because Achiever types were diehard rule keepers. Sometimes, after years of rigid rule-following, their inner rebel often reared up and broke a big no-no rule in a big way.

Did her shadow rebel talk her into murder? Unlikely. It'd been fourteen years since Marie had stolen Sarah's boyfriend. Even if she still gossiped about it, she was now happy with her fiancé.

Sarah checked her watch. "Better get started on the sandwiches. We always get a few customers when we open."

"Not sure anyone will show up for afternoon tea today," Annie said.

Rose sniffed as she reached for a tray. "How come I don't smell meat pies? Didn't Mrs. O'Grady want some for her event?"

"She canceled a while ago." Kirsten attacked the onion with a knife and diced so fast I feared she'd cut off a finger.

Rose's tray landed with a thump on the counter. "Holy big deal. She's invited fifty guests. How's she going to feed them all?"

My mind homed in on the word *invited*, like on GG's personal invitation to Annie's Lemon Delight Event. "Meg Twist's invite had her name on it. Since you didn't invite Marie, how did she get one?"

"I don't know because I made it an invitation-only event so Marie wouldn't show up." Annie threw her arms up. "And look how that turned out."

"Marie had the postcard invite, not the personalized letter one," Rose said.

"There were two versions?" I said.

"Yes." Annie strode to the small desk in the corner, pulled a card out of a file folder and returned to the counter. "I had fifty of these made for us to give to friends. Somehow Marie got a hold of one."

I plucked it out of her hand and stared at the lemon-yellow postcard. I closed my eyes to grasp a niggly thought at the edge of my consciousness.

"What is it, Madame Mystic?" Rose asked.

Kirsten snorted. "Her handsome, hulky spirit guide has probably sent her another vision."

Rats. So hard to focus with all the chef's snarky comments. I opened my eyes. "Something about this invite..." I held it as if I could pick up some telltale vibe.

"What does your handsome spirit guide look like?" Rose asked, her voice dreamy. "Mine is a skinny, old man with teeth as long as his ratty gray hair. Nice guy, though."

Kirsten, knife in hand, pointed it at me. "Yeah, what does your hulky spirit guy look like?"

An image of Jake popped into my head with his cropped, short dark brown hair, two days of beard growth, and his eyes, those expressive slate grays. I pushed his image away to conjure up someone who looked different. The gorgeous Viking man from the fair appeared.

"He's tall, rugged, has thick blond hair and dark blue eyes. Very Viking-like. Oh, and he's got a mermaid tattoo on his left bicep."

Everyone went hold-your-breath still. Kirsten's knife clanked on the floor. Annie's eyes grew as big as watermelons.

"Not funny," Sarah said.

Uh-oh. "What?" I asked.

Rose gave a nervous giggle. "Your spirit guide looks just like Michael Larson, Sarah's fiancé."

Chapter 12

MY BRAIN STALLED FOR a beat. The gorgeous Viking guy was Sarah's fiancé. I'd lived in the anonymity of Boston for too long. Of course, an attractive man like Michael would not go unnoticed in a small town. He must have moved to town after I left.

A few pieces of Marie's murder puzzle slowly clicked into place.

"He's just one of my spirit guides." I scrambled for British terms. "And blimey, he's rather a brilliant chameleon. The bloke changes his looks to match the cryptic message he wants to send me."

"Really," Kirsten drawled as she reached for another onion.

I held the yellow postcard to the side of my face. "I sense this invite has a message for me." I swung a mystic-like gaze to Sarah. "You were at the fair on Saturday with your fiancé."

"Yes, for a while before Michael went to work. Then I met up with Kirsten and Rose."

Something in her words felt out of place but eluded me as the potent diced onions made my eyes water. "I see you three together at a hotdog cart."

The three women gaped at me.

"Wow," Rose said. "We met for lunch before Sarah and I went to work."

"How did you know that?" Sarah asked me.

"A good guess," Kirsten said, but a flicker of uncertainty rippled across her face before it settled back into an expression of pure cynicism.

Such a lot of work to convince the chef my fake powers came straight from the mystic world. It was tough to fool the Leader types, who, although great at dishing out lies, also had built-in lie detectors.

I shifted my attention to Sarah. "You hated Marie."

"Who didn't?"

Wow. No one even tried to deny their hate-on for Marie.

When she and Michael were flirting and talking, Sarah appeared, claimed her man then handed Marie the yellow postcard to a competitor's event she'd want to attend.

A well-planned murder—invite Marie to the Lemon Delight Event and ensure she ate a poisoned tart. How fortuitous Annie had insisted on giving Marie the test tarts, after which Sarah could've easily swapped the two leftover test tarts with poisoned ones.

Now to trick her into a confession. With the invite against my temple, I said, "Blimey, here's another vision. I see Sarah giving Marie an invite to this event."

Everyone gasped. Sarah drew back. Her horrified expression looked real. "I did not."

I might've believed her if I didn't have irrefutable proof she did. Before I reached for my purse, I paused for a moment. They'd know I didn't divine the image if I showed them the photo. My fake psychic cover would be history, and it was such a great way to remain incognito in Shadow Falls until the statute of limitations had passed.

I swayed and searched for another angle. I'd ruled out Sarah because her dislike for Marie stemmed from an incident fourteen years ago about a boyfriend she no longer cared about. But what if...I thrust out my arm and pointed the card at her. "Marie stole your boyfriend in high school."

Sarah's hand flew to her mouth.

I slapped the invite up to my temple, closed my eyes and slowed the tempo of my voice. "Not just your boyfriend. Marie had this superpower over the boys. She'd flirt with them until they dumped their girlfriends, and then she moved on. Her success rate was over the moon high."

My eyes flew open so fast it startled Sarah, and she reared back.

"I see Marie and your fiancé. She's touching his mermaid tattoo, leaning in close, batting her eyelashes, flirting up a storm strong enough to start a tsunami. Or steal a fiancé."

"Holy psychic," Rose muttered. "Madame Mystic's spot on."

I thrust the invite in the air between us. "You'd do anything to stop Marie from stealing another man from you. Even murder. You hatched the idea when you saw the poison label on the lemon oil bottle."

"I did not."

"Okay. When did you get the idea?"

She stomped her right foot. "I did not poison Marie."

The other women shifted their gazes to me. Kirsten's look clearly said, *what are you going to do now?*

Drat. Why didn't Sarah spew out a confession as criminals did on TV cop shows?

"Hello," a woman called from the kitchen door.

Heather Towers. A tall, thin woman who loved the color pink. Her pink trench coat hung open revealing a white blouse and pink jeans. Three other women crowded in behind her. I recognized all of them as members of the town's garden club.

"Hello, Heather," Annie said.

"Oh." The president of the club turned as pink as her coat. "We thought you'd still be in jail."

"I'm out on bail."

"I see. Well, the garden club thought... I mean, we voted and..." Heather visibly swallowed. "The vote was unanimous. We want our deposit check back. We've decided to use a catering company from Canandaigua."

"I understand," Annie said, all business polite. "I'll mail you a check."

"We want the check now," someone behind Heather said.

Annie flinched.

"Listen up, you wankers," I said, reveling in my disguise, "Annie did not poison anyone."

Kirsten snarled and stabbed an onion with her knife. "Yeah. And anyone who thinks so is an idiot."

I smiled. Always good to have a Leader type on your side.

All four garden club members stiffened but didn't respond. Their gazes fixated on the knife as they shifted back in unison.

"Kirsten. Oli—" Annie coughed. "Madame Mystic. It's okay."

Yikes. She'd almost called me Olivia.

Annie bobbed her head at the women. "My checkbook is in my office. Be back in a minute." She lifted her chin, threw back her shoulders and left the kitchen.

Kirsten yanked the knife out of the onion.

"Don't, Kirsten," Sarah said.

The chef whirled, knife in hand. "Don't what?"

"Now, Kirsten," Rose said in a soothing voice.

"We'll wait outside." Heather's voice came out in a squeak.

The women spilled out of the kitchen and closed the door behind them.

The chef glared at her co-workers. "What did you think I would do with this knife?"

Sarah and Rose exchanged glances. When Leader types get angry and aggressive, they look downright scary.

"Ladies," I said, "let's all take a calming breath."

Surprisingly, they did, even the knife-wielding chef.

Annie, check in hand, strode into the kitchen. "Where's Heather and the others?"

Rose and Sarah looked at Kirsten. She shrugged her shoulders.

"They wanted to wait outside."

Annie opened the kitchen door and handed one of the ladies the check. She closed the door and rested her forehead on it. "The garden club's annual fundraiser is a huge chunk of business for me."

She turned anguished eyes to her staff. "I'll have to close the diner if another big customer cancels an event."

The three women exchanged worried glances.

It'd take weeks before Annie went to trial, but she didn't have weeks to save her business. The next phone call might be the cancellation catalyst for closing up shop.

Time to figure out which of her staff killed Marie. Since Sarah had not yet confessed, I needed to try another tactic. "Sarah."

"What?"

"When Marie arrived at the Lemon Delight event, you asked Annie if you should retrieve the test tarts. When she said, 'no,' you looked disappointed. Why?"

"Because…" she sighed. "Because I hated it when Marie flirted with Michael. I'll admit I wanted to shove one of those disgusting tarts down her throat." Sarah waggled the ring finger showcasing her engagement ring. "I didn't poison her because Michael loves me. He asked me to marry him two weeks ago."

Kirsten snorted. "You're crazy for trusting him."

"I am not."

"Kirsten," Annie chided and cast a look of pity at Sarah.

So did Rose before her gaze dropped to the floor.

Ah. It seemed Sarah's coworkers all agreed on one thing. I hesitated, then decided not to sugarcoat her feelings, especially since she'd framed my friend. "I sense Michael isn't faithful to you."

Uncertainty rippled across her face as she twisted her apron into a wrinkled mess. "Yes, he is. And I did not give Marie an invite or poison her."

Achiever types did not twist clothing into wrinkled messes unless under severe stress. Was Sarah uncertain about Michael's fidelity, or was she lying about poisoning Marie? Maybe both.

My hand shook as I placed the invite on the counter. To save Annie from a murder charge, I needed to blow my psychic cover and risk getting hauled off to jail.

Chapter 13

IF I SHOWED THEM the photo of Sarah handing Marie the invite, they'd know I was a fake psychic and wonder about my identity. Sarah wouldn't take long to remember Olivia Twist from high school, especially with all the time sitting in a jail cell.

I opened my purse to retrieve my phone, prepared to show them the incriminating picture. An idea popped up. If it worked, I'd keep Madame Mystic alive.

"Annie." I closed my purse and slung it over my shoulder. "A word, please. In your office."

"Ohhhhh," Kirsten drawled. "Did your spirits fly off when they realized they were just a figment of your imagination?"

I ignored her and focused on my friend.

"Okay," Annie said. "Ladies, please start on the sandwiches for afternoon tea. Just make half the usual amount. We'll probably only get a few tourists today." She nodded toward the pie shells. "Kirsten, please bake those pies. I'll put them on sale for half price."

I glanced at Annie's purse on the small desk as we left the kitchen. Hopefully, her cell phone hadn't run out of juice.

We walked through the diner and down the hallway to a small

windowless office.

With barely enough space for a desk and a chair, she'd squeezed in a five-tiered plastic shelf stocked with paper towels, toilet paper and napkins.

"Was this a closet?" I asked.

"Yes, a supply closet. If I close the door, it gets claustrophobic."

Time to get cozy. I shut the door, retrieved my phone and enlarged the photo to show the yellow postcard. "Here." I handed over my phone. "Sarah's handing it to Marie. I didn't realize until just now it was one of your invites."

Annie peered at the screen. "Olivia, why didn't—"

"Call me Madame Mystic."

"Why didn't you just show us the picture instead of faking a vision of it?"

"I need to build up my reputation as a psychic. And I thought my vision might startle Sarah into a confession."

Annie tsked. "Murderers in real life don't confess like they do on television."

One arrest, and she'd become an expert. "Here's the plan. I'll text you the picture. When we return to the kitchen, you get your phone to check messages. I'll start another fake psychic vision, and you interrupt me to say someone just texted you the picture."

"Like who?"

"Anyone. It doesn't matter."

She beamed and handed back my phone. "A jolly good plan."

"Indeed, it is. First, let's make sure..." I leaned against the door and held up my phone. Not far enough away, I raised my arm high. "Back up. Can you tell this is your invite?"

Her chair scraped the floor. "Yes, old bean, I can."

"Let's leave the British to Madame Mystic, shall we?" I texted her the picture and opened the door. "Back to the kitchen. For this to work, I must pretend a psychic vision first."

She nodded, and we returned to the kitchen.

"I better check my phone for messages." Annie's announcement ricocheted off the walls as she reached for her purse.

Wow. So far from subtle.

Rose and Sarah exchanged glances over their cheese sandwich production.

"Glad you're keeping us informed," Kirsten said, spreading meringue over lemon filling in a pie.

Annie flushed as she looked at her phone. "I haven't checked since yesterday. Oh, some texts from friends who want to know how I survived my night in jail."

I gasped, threw my arm straight out and stumbled toward the counter as if some invisible force dragged me. I stopped where I'd tossed the invite, picked it up and slapped it against my temple.

"Saaaarah," I called out in a ghost-like voice.

"Oh, jeez. What?"

"The vision is so clear now that my head hurts. You gave Marie an invite to the event."

Sarah smacked the counter. "I did not."

Kirsten groaned. "I thought we covered this already."

I closed my eyes. "I see it as if it's a movie. The vision has zoomed in on Marie's stall at the fair. Oh, it's at the end of a row. Michael is there. Marie puts her hand on his mermaid tattoo. He laughs at—"

"Oh, Madame Mystic," Annie interrupted in a sing-song voice.

I opened one eye. "Yes?"

She stared down at her phone. How did she make her face go so pale? Good acting.

I expected her to launch into her someone-sent-me-a-picture-of-Sarah-at-the-fair speech, but instead, she said, "I think your spirit guide sent me a text."

Sheesh. Why hadn't she used a real person's name? Whoever heard of a spirit guide texting?

"What is the message?" I sing-songed back.

"It's…" Annie bit her lip. "It's in a mystic language that I don't understand."

Huh? I moved to stand in front of her, my back to the others. "What is it?"

She turned her phone toward me. "See," she proclaimed while she made the image of Sarah in the incriminating photo bigger. "A message I can't interpret."

For the first time, I looked closely at the woman who'd claimed Michael before she'd handed Marie the postcard.

My mouth dropped open. A series of mental images flashed like an old-fashioned slide show.

Earlier, when I'd divined Sarah and Michael together at the fair, she'd said, *For a while before Michael went to work. Then I met up with Kirsten and Rose.*

Something about what she'd said didn't quite fit. Now I knew why. Timing. I'd seen the three women together at the hotdog cart *before* seeing Marie with Michael.

The final pieces of Marie's murder puzzle clicked into place as if guided by a mystic force. Goosebumps coated my body.

I spun, strode to the counter and pointed the invite at Sarah. "Earlier, you said you were with Michael at the fair *before* he went to work, right?"

"Yes." She cut the crusts off another cheese sandwich and muttered, "If this psychic crackpot accuses me of murder again, I'll quit."

"It was a test." I whirled and pointed the card at Kirsten. "And *you* failed! How can you stand by and let me accuse your friend of murder when it was you who poisoned Marie?"

"OMG." Kirsten fisted her hips. "Now you've circled back to me."

"You read Annie's journal and saw what she'd written beside Marie's name."

"Rose found the journal and showed us. All of us. Tell her, Rose."

Her freckles darkened as she sheepishly nodded.

I edged closer to Kirsten. "And you ran with the idea."

She gripped her spatula. "We've gone through this. When Marie fired me, she did me a favor because Annie hired me. Are you sure your spirit guides aren't all liquored up?"

"No, sober as the supreme court."

Sarah tsked. "The supreme court is a location. It can't—"

"That's not why you offed Marie." I waved the invite and stared Kirsten straight in the eyes. "You'd heard about her flirty superpowers and how she stole other women's men. And you were afraid she'd steal Michael."

Like most Leader types, the chef was a great actress—not even a flinch.

"Why would I kill Marie because she stole another woman's fiancé?"

"Yeah, why would she do that?" Rose shook her head as she lifted a tray of sandwiches. "I'll take these to the refrigerator."

Sarah snagged a quarter of a cheese sandwich from the tray as Rose passed her. "Maybe you should change your name to Madame Mystic-Less."

I ignored their comments and focused on Kirsten.

"You weren't afraid Marie would steal Michael from Sarah. You were afraid she'd steal Michael from you."

Chapter 14

KIRSTEN SWALLOWED AND WITHDREW a step. "You're crazy. There's nothing between Michael and me." But her voice and posture had lost enough oomph for the others to doubt her.

Sarah froze, her teeth clamped on a sandwich.

Rose whirled. Quarter-cut sandwiches flew off the tray. Pieces of cheese, lettuce leaves, tomato slices and bread dotted the floor. No one reached for them.

I placed the invite against my right temple. "After the three of you ate lunch, Sarah and Rose left for work. You wandered around the fair. Perhaps Sarah had told you Michael was at work, or perhaps he'd told you."

I fake frowned. "Terribly sorry, but the spirits aren't clear. Either way, Michael lied. He did not go to work. He met up with Marie, and she was all over him like one of the queen's dogs on a royal bone."

Sarah let out a sob. The sandwich fell out of her mouth, bounced off her chest and hit the floor.

Kirsten had no trouble expressing outrage at something she thought unfair, like when Marie had fired her. However, she couldn't express anger at Marie for stealing her man when that man was engaged to someone else. Kirsten had to bury her rage, and buried rage always leaks out in some way.

"A fortnight ago," I continued, "Michael asked Sarah to marry him. Perhaps you were okay with this."

I frowned again. "Perhaps not. Either way, he still wanted to see you on the side. But he's only a two-woman man. You knew if Marie got her hooks into Michael, he'd toss you away like rubbish."

Kirsten's mouth opened and closed while she struggled to regain her oomph. She straightened and smirked. "Too bad psychic visions aren't accepted as proof in a court of law."

Annie let out a loud, fake gasp. "This picture someone just texted me is proof."

She held her phone up and maneuvered around scattered sandwiches to Kirsten. "It's quite clear. You gave Marie an invite to the event."

"I'm surprised she didn't question your reason why," I mused. "You'd called her a snarly hag in public."

Recalling how Marie had smiled and accepted the postcard, I tapped the invite against my temple. "I sense you gave her a fake apology, followed by this gift."

The color drained from Kirsten's cheeks as she stared at the photo.

Still holding the tray, Rose moved closer to look at the incriminating picture. So did Sarah. Her hand flew to her chest. "Oh, no."

The chef laid her spatula on the counter and gazed at her boss. "Annie, I'm sorry. I never meant to implicate you." She pivoted to bolt.

Rose swung the tray and clipped Kirsten across the head.

She fell against the counter and lunged for the chef's knife. She righted herself and brandished the blade. "Stay back. All of you." Feeling her way along the counter with her other hand, her eyes, wild with fear, darted from one to another.

Bloody buckets of bones. I had no doubt Kirsten would stab

anyone who went near her. Once we were out of knife reach, I'd call the sheriff. "Let her go."

"Yes," Annie agreed. "I don't want anyone to get hurt."

"Not a chance." Sarah slipped her right palm under a pie plate, brought her arm back then tossed it as a professional pitcher might.

The pie sailed through the air and hit the murderess square in the face. The dish and crust slid to the floor. Kirsten reached up, grabbed a fistful of pie and flung it back at us.

"Oh, blimey." I dropped the glob-covered invite.

"I'm calling the sheriff." Annie wiped off her phone with her sleeve.

Too busy swiping at her lemon-meringue-filled eyes with her knife-free hand, Kirsten didn't see Sarah pick up another pie and round the counter.

Rose dropped the tray and clamped her hand on a pie. She flung it like a frisbee. It sailed past the chef, landed right side up on the floor and skidded a few feet before it slowed to a stop.

"Oh, nuts." The redhead scooped up another pie.

Sarah smashed the second pie hard into her fiancé-stealing ex-friend's face. Kirsten dropped the knife in her attempt to stay upright.

Rose arrived and shoved another pie into her face. The chef toppled over and landed on her back with a thump. She groaned as she rolled to a seated position.

I scanned the pie-spattered floor. Where was the knife?

"Stay right where you are!" Rose persuaded Kirsten to stay still with the point of the large chef's knife.

"Can you find something to tie her up with?" I asked Sarah.

Like a well-oiled crime machine, she whipped off her apron and used the ties as a rope to secure Kirsten's hands behind her back.

Annie covered the mouthpiece of her phone. "Rose, please stick a note on the front door canceling the high tea this afternoon."

"I'll take that," I said, carefully taking the knife from Rose's shaking hands.

She wobbled over to the sink to wash her hands first.

"Hello, Sheriff," Annie said with a self-satisfied smirk. "Just wondering if you have time to come to the diner and arrest Marie Holinder's murderer?"

The smirk slid off her face. "No, this is not a confession."

Chapter 15

THREE HOURS AFTER ANNIE'S charges were dropped, she texted me: **Going to Florida. Only way to stop my folks from coming home. Back in a month.**

I texted back: **What about the diner?**

Rose and Sarah running it.

A month. Good. I needed the time. I had a long conversation with GG and told her what I wanted to do with a portion of the money she'd set aside for what she called the ORP—Olivia Redemption Project. At first, she rejected my idea until I swayed her with a rational explanation.

Generous Granny set up a business account in her name and gave me access. She transferred five thousand dollars to the ORP account to use at my discretion as a slush fund and only wanted to approve large purchases.

GG then dug out her sewing machine and created several colorful outfits for Madame Mystic. Wearing a wig, star-shaped glasses and wild, wacky clothes is a great way to hide in plain sight.

I bought a new burner phone. I'd thrown the one with the incriminating photo in the back of the toilet before the sheriff got to the diner to arrest Kirsten and question us—to help keep Madame Mystic alive as a psychic genius. I called my roommate and left a message with my new phone number.

Two days after Kirsten's arrest, I made an appointment for the kitten with a veterinarian, old Doc Saunders. Dressed in a Garish Granny creation—a bright red, long peasant dress dotted with tiny white flowers and several beaded necklaces, I arrived on time.

It felt awkward introducing myself to people I already knew. The vet's receptionist was his wife, a heavy-set woman who radiated warmth. Mrs. Saunders beamed at me. "Oh, I love your outfit."

Was she kidding me? "Really?"

"Yes, where did you get it?"

"It's a...one of a kind."

"Too bad." She led me to the examination room. "Honey, this is Madame Mystic. She's from England and staying with Meg Twist for a while."

The Doc's shock of white hair stuck out like a porcupine who'd quilled up. "How is Meg? We've known her since grade school."

"She's peachy," I said. "Very kind of her to let me stay. Very kind, indeed."

Mrs. Saunders left, and I removed the kitten from the carrier and set it on the examination table. The little one tentatively sniffed the surface.

The vet whistled. "Well, I'll be a monkey's uncle. It's Mrs. Turner's missing Cornish Rex kitten."

Oh, no. I already thought of the kitten as mine. I clutched at my beads. "Are you sure? I found it—"

"Him."

"I found him down by the falls."

"Sounds about right. Mrs. Turner's son Bobby and his friend skipped school on Tuesday afternoon. They snuck him out of the house and went to the falls, where they got sidetracked by a snake and forgot about this little guy."

Even though my heart was cracking in half, I remembered to sprinkle in some British. "What a couple of wankers."

"Bobby's a handful and a half. Mrs. Turner and the boys looked for him until dark. When did you find him?"

"Tuesday afternoon."

Doc Saunders rubbed his bristled chin. "Sometime after the boys left and before Mrs. Turner returned with the search party. Good thing, not sure if he'd have survived a cold night."

I picked up the kitten and cuddled him into my chest. He meowed in protest. "Maybe it isn't the same kitten."

The vet's kind, brown eyes filled with pity. "I'm sorry, this is Smokey."

I considered bolting with the kitten but came up with a better idea. Hopefully, a win-win one. "Will you call Mrs. Turner now and let me speak to her?"

"Sure."

After tucking Smokey into the carrier, I followed the vet to the reception area, where he placed the call. He cringed when Mrs. Turner's squeals of delight blasted from the phone. "The woman who found Smokey is Madame Mystic, and she wants to talk to you." He handed me the receiver.

"Hello, Mrs. Turner."

"Thank you so much," she said. "Is Smokey okay?"

"Yes. Jolly happy I found him. He's so small and helpless. I hope your son doesn't sneak him out again."

"Eight-year-old boys. What a pack of trouble. He promised he'd never do it again." She sighed.

I figured her sigh meant she couldn't trust him. "Perchance, do you want to sell the kitten? I'm quite taken with him, and I don't have children. He'd be quite *safe* with me."

"I'm not sure...maybe. My husband was mad at how much I paid for him."

My heart leaped, and I gripped the receiver. "I'll give you a hundred dollars for him."

She snickered. "I paid eight hundred."

I blinked. "Really?"

"Yes. I tell you what. Give me twelve hundred. It'll cover my vet costs and the raw cat food I stocked up on, which you can take."

If I bought the kitten, I'd use up a chunk of the startup money GG had transferred to my business account. For sure, she'd turn into Grumpy Granny. But to leave him in a house with a forgetful, untrustworthy little boy who preferred the company of snakes? I shuddered. No way. "Sold."

After arranging for the exchange, Doc updated the microchip ID with Meg Twist's contact information. He checked over the kitten and pronounced him healthy. "Smokey's been neutered. Do you know much about the Cornish Rex breed?"

"No, but I'll read up on them."

"This breed is quite active and can jump higher than your garden variety of domestic cats."

"I've noticed." The kitten nudged my hand, and I stroked his ear. "Meg does get appalled every time this rascal leaps onto the kitchen counter."

"Some folks call them half dogs because they aren't your typical cat. They give and need a lot of affection. They'll follow you around. Oh, and another thing—"

His words faded into the background as worry nagged at me. How did I break it to GG that I used twelve hundred dollars to buy what she called a rat-like creature? The one she'd forbidden me to keep in her home.

Doc stopped talking when his wife stuck her head in the examination room and announced his next appointment.

I'd just placed the cat carrier in the back seat of my car when Vivian, my roommate, called me.

"I've got exciting news," she said. "I'm moving to Chicago because I got the nutritionist position. I start in a month."

"Great. Can you use personality profiling like you wanted to?"

"Whatever helps my clients lose weight."

"Although I'll miss you, I'm happy for you."

When we discovered both of us had a loved one presumed dead in the Middle East, we'd spent many an evening at a local bar where we nursed glasses of white wine and talked about them.

I'd talked about Jake, how I couldn't move on. She'd talked about her only sibling Sam, how he'd raised her, how she'd hated it when he wore goofy ties. And how she'd give anything again to see him wearing one.

Then after a toast to their safe return, we'd used our new-found knowledge of the five main life-purpose personalities to read people and fabricate stories about their lives. Vivian was better than me because she had more experience. Her brother had taught her the dark sides of the personality types long before she'd signed up to learn about the light sides.

"I'll especially miss our game," I said.

"We had some great times, Olivia." Her tone held a hint of sadness. "Sorry to bail on you. Do you want to take over the lease on the apartment?"

I'd never confessed my mini crime spree to Vivian. Her right-eous indignation for anything on the wrong side of legal was both admirable and annoying. She'd stopped talking to her brother when she learned he was a thief. Even though he only stole from people who'd stolen from others, she wanted nothing to do with him—until he went missing in the Middle East.

Although we'd bonded talking about our missing loved ones, Vivian had no idea why I'd moved in with her—to stay off the paper-trail grid.

As it turned out, despite her love of everything yellow, her messiness, and her need to give unsolicited advice, we clicked as roommates. She was my favorite friend after Annie.

"I'm moving back—"

"Oh, hold on," Vivian said, "someone's at the door. I'll call you back." She hung up.

I closed the back-passenger door and rounded my car to the driver's side.

A white car with blue stripes and the word Sheriff painted in giant letters on the door pulled to a stop beside me. Trevor rolled down the window. "Hello, Vivian."

I swallowed. "I'd prefer if you call me Madame Mystic."

He nodded, exited his car, leaned against it and crossed his arms. "Did you find your phone?"

I didn't want him to ask for my new phone number. "Not yet."

He studied me. "Funny how someone with a burner phone texted Annie an incriminating photo *before* your mystic revelation."

"I told you I didn't see the photo on Annie's phone until after I divined it." Technically true. I'd seen the photo, but not on Annie's phone.

"Uh-huh." He opened the door, climbed into his car and stuck his head out the window. "Kirsten Olson went for a plea deal to get the charge dropped to second-degree murder. You won't need to go to court."

I tried not to let my relief show. "Oh, I've never been a witness before."

He tipped his hat. "Thanks for—" he cleared his throat "—your psychic help."

I knew he knew I wasn't psychic. "You're welcome."

"I heard a rumor you're moving to Shadow Falls."

I smiled. "It's true. I'm renting a room from Meg Twist."

"Good day." He drove off.

I waved. "Bye, Sheriff." I'd need to stay out of his way.

If I'd gone to a court as a witness, one of the lawyers would've asked me to state my real name. Better look into the legalities of using a fake name. Better also let Vivian know I'd used her name before she found out from the sheriff's office.

I dug out my new phone and slid into the back seat of my car to let the kitten out of the carrier. He hopped into the driver seat, stood on his hind legs, put his paws on the steering wheel and sniffed.

I called Vivian.

"Just about to call you back," she said, her voice high-pitched with excitement. "Guess who knocked on my door?"

"Ah—"

"I'll give you a hint. He wore a goofy tie, a baby blue one covered with little neon yellow ducklings."

I gasped. "Your brother Sam."

"Yes, he'd been captured, just like—"

"I'm so happy Sam is back, but I need to tell you something sooner rather than later."

"Oh?"

I sighed and told her everything, starting with why I'd left Shadow Falls. "I'm moving back here, and for the next year, I'm incognito as Madame Mystic."

"How dare you use my name as a fake psychic?" Vivian's voice, already tight with fury, turned into a shriek. "Why didn't you pick another profession? You know how I feel about those thieving crackpots."

"Because Annie needed a tea leaf reader. I'm sorry, I panicked and used your name."

"I can't talk to you right now." She hung up.

I sighed. My redemption list just got longer.

Chapter 16

THE MORNING AFTER ANNIE got home from Florida, she called me. "I'm so glad to be home. Florida's too hot in May. Any news about Kirsten?"

I told Annie what the sheriff had told me.

She whistled. "I heard Sarah broke it off with Michael. Smart move."

"Yeah. What are you up to now? I want to show you something."

"What?" she asked.

"It's a surprise."

"Ooh, I like surprises. Come on over."

Gray clouds loomed overhead, so I wore my new weather-proof coat. Five minutes later, I showed up at Annie's parents' home, two streets over from GG's, and parked beside her catering van.

At the front door, she greeted me with a smile then eyeballed my coat and shoes. "Nice heels, nice coat, but you hate red."

"Everyone knows Olivia Twist thinks red and other bright colors are too flamboyant to wear whereas Madame Mystic fancies a bright, cheery color."

Annie fingered the collar of my coat. "Gorgeous material. Isn't this too trendy an outfit for Madame Mystic?"

I unbuttoned my coat to reveal the embroidered smock dress underneath. "How about this?"

She grimaced. "Where'd you buy that?"

"GG made it for me. Grab your coat and umbrella. It might rain."

"Where are we going?" She checked her watch. "Sarah and Rose are at the diner to prep, and then they're off. I open at two."

"It's not even noon yet. Come on."

We made it into the car just as it started to drizzle.

"How's the kitten?" Annie asked as we settled into our seats.

By the time I'd updated her on my new kitten adventures, we'd crossed over the bridge. I navigated the slick road down the escarpment. "Can you believe Mrs. Turner called him Smokey? How cliché."

"What did you name him?"

"I named him Shadow after our hometown and because he follows me everywhere."

"Ah, way more unique for a gray cat."

"A gray and white cat."

"A lot more gray than white. If you want a cat so bad, why pay so much money? Why not a rescue cat?"

"Animals who aren't rescues need homes, too. And technically, this little guy got rescued, first from a for-sure death by freezing, then from a boy who prefers snakes. I'll get a rescue playmate for Shadow."

"Ooh, good idea."

"Wonder if he likes dogs," I said. "I've always wanted a cat and a dog."

When we reached the downtown strip, I parked my old car on the lot by the lake. We exited and raised our umbrellas to ward off the misty rain, then I guided Annie across the road and stopped at the old video store. "Here we are."

She gaped up at the large, cherry-red letters painted in a mystic-type font on the new sign above the entrance to the store.

"What do you think?" I asked.

"Madame Mystic's Emporium?" Her gaze shifted to the Bristol board sign I'd propped against one of the interior bay windows. It read, *Opening Soon.*

She turned to me. "What's going on?"

"I need to run a legitimate business as Madame Mystic. It'll help me with my cover."

"An emporium is a place where they sell a lot of things. Why don't you just focus on one thing?"

"Because, Annie, I've discovered I'm a multi-potentialist."

Her face scrunched. "A what?"

"A multi-potentialist. It's someone who needs variety, or they die of boredom." I held up my right hand, fingers splayed. "I plan to sell five things. Psychic Tea Leaf Readings, Gently Used Books, Vintage DVDs because an unopened box came with the place—"

"Why not palm or card reading?"

"Because I can gaze into a clump of wet tea leaves and say whatever I want. I don't know how to read Tarot Cards."

Annie tilted her head. "You'll need to serve tea. Why not gaze into a crystal ball?"

Because I've got a much better idea. "Hmmm. Something to consider. And I'll sell One-of-a-Kind Clothing. GG will make them. I've started a trend with my Madame Mystic clothing."

"You're delusional."

"The vet's wife loved my outfit. And I ran into Nurse Nancy's mother last week. She loved my smock. Wanted to know where I bought it."

"She's ninety and half-blind." Annie raised a finger one at a time. "Fake tea leaf readings, smelly old books, DVDs no one even wanted back in the day and ugly clothing. What's the fifth thing you won't sell to anyone?"

Ah, she'd learned from recent events. "Look at you. Hating

on my store right to my face."

"Sorry," she mumbled and flicked her gaze to the café bakery next door. "I heard it's indefinitely closed."

"Yeah."

The misty rain turned to splats, bouncing off the sidewalk and my new shoes. "Let's get out of this weather."

Once inside, we found a space to place our open umbrellas amongst the dismantled metal shelves, which took up most of the cracked tile floor.

"I'm almost afraid to ask," Annie said. "What's the fifth thing you want to sell?"

"Raw Pet Food."

She gaped at me. "No way."

"Yeah, way. I don't want to drive to Canandaigua every few days to buy it." I pointed to the wall on the left. "I think I'll put a double refrigerator in the middle to separate the books from the DVDs."

She surveyed the room. "This place is a mess. When do you plan to open?"

"Soon. The renovations start tomorrow. Did you know there's an apartment upstairs? Gossip Granny told me that when the previous owner and his wife divorced, she got the house, and he refurbished the upper floor and made it into an apartment."

"Probably didn't need the storage space after VHS became extinct."

I nodded. "My contractor knocked down the wall between the kitchen and living room to open it up. He installed a new stove and fridge yesterday. Still needs furniture."

Annie squinted at me. "I thought GG wanted you to live with her."

"She does. I convinced GG we'd get more money for rent if I updated the apartment. At first, she said no, because she thought I'd use it." I shrugged. "I might on the odd night. Come see."

We picked our way through the scattered debris to the stairs.

"How many years before you try to find a renter?" Annie asked as we got close to the top.

My heart warmed. There's one thing money can never buy—a friend who's known you most of your life.

I laughed. "I've already lined one up."

"Who?"

"I'll tell you soon." My stomach grumbled. "I'm hungry. Want some lunch?"

She bit her lip. "Are you going to make me talk about what happened?"

"You promised." I grasped the knob on the apartment door.

"Wait. Let me say it now."

"Okay."

She let out a long breath. "First, thank you for getting me off the murder charge, but..."

"But what?"

"I'm still angry at you for stealing from me." Her eyes welled. "How could you do that to me? I trusted you. You betrayed me." Her voice, so small, sounded no older than a five-year-old's.

With a good chunk of the Creative personality in her, chances were she'd never get in-your-face outraged with anyone. At least, not on her behalf, but she'd just faced a live person and spoken the truth of her anger. Maybe she'd get to the point where she no longer needed her journal.

"I am so sorry," I said. "You don't know how many times I've wished time travel was real so I could go back and change everything."

"What happened? Why did you steal from us?"

"Raymond Teller happened. He's the guy who recruited me to sell the Erase & Smooth skincare line. He convinced me I'd earn a whack more money if I put together my own team. You weren't interested, but I recruited seven others. They each paid me one thousand dollars for a start-up kit of samples to give to potential clients."

"I heard." Annie tsked. "Every one of them called to ask me where you were after you skipped town."

Guilt bit at me. "They're all on my redemption list." I opened the door. "I'll tell you the rest over lunch."

We stepped inside the apartment. A few scattered cat toys littered the freshly stained hardwood floor of the otherwise empty room.

"Wow. It's beautiful." Annie sniffed. "I can still smell the paint.

"Thanks. The contractor finished the floors and walls a few days ago. Put your coat on one of those hooks near the door."

Shadow came in from the bedroom and stretched into a downward dog pose.

"Shadow," Annie squealed, picked him up and nuzzled him. "You're into yoga. And you've grown. Still adorable as ever."

He meowed. It might've meant, finally, someone else sees how cute I am.

"Wait." Annie squinted at me. "Why is Shadow here? Is he your new renter?"

"He's agreed to look for mice and let me cuddle him as payment."

"Does GG know?"

"She knows I found him a new home."

Annie placed Shadow on the floor and rounded on me. "You're deceiving Generous Granny after all she's done for you?"

"I'm kidding. GG knows he lives at the emporium, where I'll spend a lot of my time. And I do have a line on a renter." I moved toward the kitchen. "Want some of GG's homemade pea soup?"

"Sure, after I call the diner." Annie disappeared into the bedroom.

A few minutes later, she wandered back. "Even though everyone knows I didn't poison Marie, no one wants to buy my lemon meringue pies anymore."

"No surprise there." Hopefully, she'd like my solution for her. "Soup's ready."

She settled on a stool at the counter, snagged a slice of fresh baguette and buttered it while I ladled the soup. I set the bowls on the counter and removed Shadow from the other stool. He meowed in protest.

"This soup is yummy," Annie said.

I dug in and wolfed down half the soup before I reached for a baguette slice.

"Time for the rest of your story," Annie said. "What happened after you recruited your sales team to sell the skincare line?"

I buttered the bread as I gnawed on my lower lip. Although I'd begged Annie for a chance to explain, I now realized it'd lead me right to where I did not want to go.

Chapter 17

Maybe if I diverted Annie's attention, often easy to do with a Creative personality type, she might forget I'd wanted a chance to explain the theft. "Remember when we were younger, how we talked about living next door to each other after we both got married?"

"Yes, on a cul-de-sac." Annie's eyes flew open. "Ooh, did Generous Granny buy us side-by-side houses?"

"No. I used some of the ORP money—"

"ORP?"

"Olivia Redemption Project. I used some of the money to buy..." I paused for dramatic effect "...the café bakery."

Annie snarled, hopped to her feet and fisted her hands. "You bought the bakery! You barely know how to bake beans." Her eyes welled. "How could you betray me again?"

Wow. When trust gets eroded, it's hard to get it back. "Again, no." I pulled a piece of paper from my purse. "Look at this."

She scanned it. Her eyes grew as big as kiwis. "Is this for real?"

"Instead of house neighbors, how about retail neighbors? You and the bank now own the café bakery. GG agreed to a large down payment on the emporium for me and the bakery for you. We've got to make enough money to pay the mortgages, but the payments are low."

Annie threw her arms around me. "Thank you." She stepped back. "Sorry, I yelled at you."

"Impressive how you showed your anger, though. Your chest even heaved."

She cracked a grin. "It did, didn't it?"

"Any idea what you'll call your new bakery café?" I asked.

She slumped onto the stool. "If sales hadn't tanked on my lemon meringue pies, I would've called it The Lemon Delight Haven Café. Now I need to come up with a new name."

"Hold that thought." I scrambled to my feet. "How about dessert?" I grabbed the two butter tarts that I'd plated earlier. "Maybe I don't know how to bake a good bean, but I made these." I set the plate on the counter. "Try one."

She leaned closer to scrutinize them. "What are they?"

"A Canadian national treasure called butter tarts."

"They kind of look like pecan tarts without the pecans. And you made them?" She picked one up.

"Yes, because we can't buy them here. Try it."

She bit off a small bite. "Mm-mmm." She took a bigger bite then polished off the rest. "Delicious."

"Forget lemon meringue," I said. "How about you sell these at...The Butter Tart Haven Café?"

She tilted her head. "I love it. With the right promotion, people will come in to taste a new type of pastry."

"And...to get a tea leaf reading from me, they will need to buy a cup of tea from you."

She thrust her arms up, victory style. "This is much better than being next-door neighbors after we both get married."

"There's one more thing." I flicked a wrist. "How about you and I rent this place? I'll cut us a great deal."

"Didn't you say GG wants—"

"You live here and let me crash at times. I'll get a cat door cut.

Shadow can wander between the store and the apartment. I'll pay his half of the rent."

"Yes. Yes. Yes. Thank you. Living here will make running between the diner and the bakery so much easier. I'll move in this weekend."

"Shadow will stay with me at GG's until then." I glanced at my watch. "You've still got time before you need to open the diner. Do you want to go see the bakery?"

"Later. I still want to hear your explanation."

My heart dipped. Unfortunately, I'd run out of diversion tactics.

Shadow hopped up on the counter, rubbed his head against my shoulder and meowed. "Oh, all right, Shadow." I stroked his giant ears. "If you insist, I'll finish the story."

"I knew it," Annie said. "Avoidance by a gifting diversion. Why? Come on, spill it."

I took a deep breath and fought the urge to run. "Remember Raymond, the guy who convinced me to recruit a team?"

Annie nodded.

"After I put a team together, Raymond suggested we meet at a seafood restaurant in Rochester. He'd bring the start-up kits and buy me lunch to celebrate. He handed me one start-up kit in the parking lot and told me to double-check the contents while he loaded my car with the other kits.

"I double-checked, and all the one thousand dollar worth of samples were in the kit, so I emailed Raymond a money transfer. After lunch, he excused himself just before the check came. I assumed he went to the restroom." I snarled. "He never returned."

"Wow. He stuck you with the bill." Annie arched an eyebrow. "Was it a seven-thousand-dollar lunch?"

The amount I'd stolen from her. I cracked a half-smile. "Almost. The creep insisted we ordered surf and turf. When I realized he'd taken off, I got suspicious, ran to my car and checked the other kits. All empty boxes."

"Blasted bananas. Did you call the skincare company?"

"First thing I did. His old boss told me he'd fired Raymond three months earlier, and they weren't responsible for the stolen money. I went to the closest police station to file a report, and an officer called the bank where I'd transferred the money."

"I bet Raymond had cleaned out his account," Annie said.

"Yup. The officer said it was unlikely they'd catch him even with a warrant out for his arrest."

Understanding rippled across Annie's face. "This was the same day I asked you to transfer money for the café down payment, wasn't it?"

Annie had gotten stuck on the wrong side of a highway closure because of an accident. She had her cell phone but didn't trust bank apps, so she'd called and asked for my help. I'd fired up my computer and transferred money from her savings to her checking account so that a check would clear for the down payment.

"Uh-huh."

"I called you in the morning that day. Hadn't you already transferred my money?"

"Yes, but I still had your account information."

"Oh, right." She flicked her wrist. "Go on."

"After I finished at the police station, I drove home in a panic. My team expected me to meet them that night to deliver their kits, and all I had were empty boxes and a sob story about how I got scammed out of their money."

"Why didn't you borrow the money from GG?"

"She was on a cruise, and I couldn't contact her to ask for the money. I remembered you had ten thousand left in your savings account."

I didn't know Annie had needed that whole amount to pay the owner for baking equipment, and because I'd taken seven thousand of it, she didn't have the money at the five o'clock closing time.

The owner used Annie's lack of funds as an excuse to cancel

the deal because Marie Holinder swooped in and offered him more money. I'd learned this days later when I'd finally listened to Annie's voicemails.

"I'm sorry." I averted my gaze and nibbled on the tart crumbs from my plate. "If I'd known you needed all the money for the sale, I wouldn't have taken it."

"You'd never stolen anything before, so why then? Why didn't you ask me? Why take it behind my back?"

Each why pounded into me. Maybe if I peppered Annie with questions, she'd stop asking me hers. "Why didn't you ask me to transfer the whole amount?"

"The owner wanted cash for the equipment, so I left the money in my savings to withdraw later. When I got to the bank and realized the money was gone, I only had fifteen minutes before the sale closed. Then it was too late to get the cash from someone else."

"When I begged for more time…" her eyes dimmed, "…he told me Marie had offered more money."

Annie tilted her head. "You haven't explained why you didn't call me to ask for the money."

And we'd now reached the place I did not want to go. "Because…" A lump the size of Canada grew in my throat. My voice dropped to a croaky whisper. "Because Jake's mother called and told me he was missing in action, presumed dead."

"Oh."

"Yeah." Shadow hopped onto my lap, stretched and touched my face with a paw.

We sat in silence for a good minute. Annie dabbed at her eyes with a napkin. "All in all, not a good day."

"No. After Mrs. O'Grady's call, I went numb. I wandered around the house. I turned on GG's radio. And can you believe it? The first song they played… 'Always Something There to Remind Me.'"

"Oh, no."

"And I knew there'd always be something to remind me of

Jake in this town. No matter where I went."

"Oh, Olivia. We've always talked about everything. Why didn't you call me?"

"Because I thought my fiancé was dead, and this powerful, uncontrollable urge to leave town hit me with the force of a category-five hurricane."

I frowned. "Funny thing, I don't remember packing a suitcase. I don't remember driving. It's like I was in Shadow Falls one second and woke up in Boston the next second."

"I called you several times."

"I didn't listen to my messages for a week, and by then, I'd spent some of the money, and you'd lost the café bakery. I was too ashamed to ask GG for the money to pay you back and afraid to call you until after I did."

Annie reached over and squeezed my forearm. "Consider your redemption debt to me all paid up."

A chunk of the four-year-old heaviness in my chest crumbled. "You have no idea how happy that makes me. I've missed you." I smiled. "I can strike you off the ORP list and move on to help another friend. Hey, why didn't you report me? I'm sure the others did."

She blinked back fresh tears. "Because I got the message about Jake, too. And I figured what you'd done might've had something to do with the news."

"Then why did you refuse to talk to me after I paid you back?"

"I still felt betrayed. And by then, Jake had been found and rescued." She jerked her head toward me. "Wait. You know they found him almost a year ago, right?"

"Yeah, GG emailed me. Said he's convalescing in Buffalo." I avoided her gaze and whispered, "How's he doing?"

"I don't know." Annie tsked. "Shortly after he returned, when I called the convalescent home, some snippy nurse told me he didn't want to talk to me."

My heart leaped. "I thought Jake refused to see me because

you'd told him what I'd done."

"Nope. He refuses to see anyone outside his immediate family."

I hadn't dated anyone in the past year, not since I'd heard he'd returned alive. "Maybe he needs more time. I'll call him again."

I ignored Annie's doubtful expression. When it came to Jake O'Grady, hope sprang forever eternal.

I got up to stack the dishes in the dishwasher. "In the meantime, I've got to figure out who on my redemption list to help next. GG said our friends need more from me than just a return of the money I stole."

Annie jumped to her feet. "Ooh, and I'll help you help them while we keep your true identity a secret. It'll be fun."

Another chunk of the hurt in my heart eased. Not the pain around Jake—that would take time while I got used to the idea he was now my ex-fiancé.

I smiled at my best friend.

Maybe, after all, I did deserve a chance at redemption. Doesn't everyone?

If you're ready for another murder caper with Olivia, GG and Annie check out *Old News and Tea-Leaf Clues:*

Reading tea leaves is no mean feat...especially for a fake psychic seeking forgiveness.

When an ex-friend asks for a reading, she begs Madame Mystic (a.k.a. Olivia Twist) to "divine" who committed an unsolved murder over a decade ago.

Impossible. Can't be done. Not with tea leaves, tarot cards or one of Olivia's new crystal balls.

Olivia has a good reason for wanting to help, so she makes a wild claim...

...she tells her ex-friend she's a psychic sleuth and will track down the killer.

Olivia drags her grandmother, her best friend Annie—a whiz at out-of-the-box ideas—and a chihuahua into the investigation to help trick the suspects into coughing up clues.

Turns out not everyone likes it when a cold case heats up. And as Olivia gets closer to the truth...the unthinkable happens, and, well...

...the debate is still on. Who should get the credit for saving Olivia—her new kitten, a crystal ball, or her best friend?

Old News and Tea-Leaf Clues is also a stand-alone story.

It's available on Amazon in eBook or print or read for FREE in Kindle Unlimited!

Have You Downloaded Your FREE Novella

A persistent grandmother. A twenty-five year old death. And a shaky clue to prove it was murder.

Just when Olivia thought she was well on her way to redemption...

...she gets hit with a request to solve an old murder by channeling the dead.

How's a good-hearted fake psychic supposed to do that?

Get a free copy of *Suspect Guests and an Unwelcome Request* at IreneJorgensen.com when you join my newsletter. You'll also get cozy email stories, opportunities for more books (mine and other authors), updates, the occasional recipe and cat picture.

A Quick Note

Hi! If you'd like my gift to you, the first Olivia, GG and Annie novella, ***Suspect Guests and an Unwelcome Request,*** I invite you to join my newsletter at IreneJorgensen.com to get your free book.

I hope you enjoyed reading *Murder Calls at Shadow Falls* as much as I enjoyed writing it. (It is a shorter book than the other in my series.)

I have a favor to ask. Please consider telling your friends about this Olivia Twist cozy mystery series.

As well, it's difficult for authors to get reviews, so I'd be very grateful if you'd post a short review on Amazon or Goodreads or email me at Irene@IreneJorgensen.com.

Thanks, Irene

Also By Irene Jorgensen

Old News and Tea-Leaf Clues
Sweet Tarts and Bitter Revenge
Fake Visions and Bad Decisions
Past Crimes and Tell-Tale Signs
Check out this cozy mystery series on Amazon.

Acknowledgments

A writer needs a community; beta readers, a graphic artist, a professional editor--to name a few.

A big whopping thank you to my beta readers, Mary Jane Gallienne and Bonnie Staring, for their time and invaluable feedback. In addition, I'd like to thank Mary Jane for her expert advice on police procedures, and Bonnie for her excellent copywriting skills and the title of this book.

I also want to thank my wonderful editor Wanda for strengthening the story.

Although Olivia Twist is a fictional character, her skill set is real. I could not have written this story without 1) learning about the five main life-purpose personalities from Rhys Thomas at the Rhys Thomas Institute and 2) further training on the power of the chakras and their shadows from Margaret Lynch Raniere's transformational programs.

And last but not least, I want to thank my family and friends for all their support.

About The Author

Irene lives in southern Ontario, Canada, with her Cornish Rex cats Razzle, Annie and Shadow. Her previous Rex, Neo, was an affectionate little guy who only bit her when hungry. (Sadly, he is no longer with us.) Some of Neo's antics are the inspiration for Olivia's cat, Shadow in this cozy mystery series.

An avid reader and daydreamer growing up, Irene spent many years in the corporate world before she finally started to write down some of her stories at the age of fifty. (It's never too late to go after a dream.)

This good-hearted fake psychic cozy mystery series is a mish-mash of some of Irene's favourite things. Friendship. Justice. Personality profiling. Shadow work. The television show Psych.

She thinks it works and hopes you do, too.

Made in United States
Orlando, FL
25 February 2024

44095063R00070